SHATTERED IMAGE
The Life and Loves of a Broken Man

a biography of

Freddie Jones

Written by
Angela Weston

First published in Great Britain in 2008
by
Poseidon Publishing
PO Box 5398
Wombourne WV5 5AA

Copyright © 2008 Fred Jones

Names, characters and related indicia are copyright and
trademark Copyright © 2008 Fred Jones

Fred Jones has asserted his moral rights
to be identified as the author

A CIP Catalogue of this book is available from
the British Library

ISBN: 978-0-9560071-0-0

All rights reserved; no part of this publication may be
reproduced or transmitted by any means, electronic,
mechanical, photocopying or otherwise without the written
permission of the publisher.

Printed and bound in
Great Britain by Biddles Ltd,
King's Lynn, Norfolk

Acknowledgments

I would like to acknowledge with the utmost gratitude, Angela Weston whose hard work and help made this biography possible from the details supplied by me, a friend of the family S.S.S whose help and legal overseeing has been a benefit which is much appreciated.

I would wish to put on record my undying thanks to the hospital staff at all the hospitals that have given me care and help, in particular, The Royal Shrewsbury Hospital and the Robert Jones and Agnes Hunt Hospital at Oswestry, without whose care and attention I would not be here. Pete Old, Stan Bloor, Dave Allen and John Sankey who saved me from certain death on 2nd April 1988.

To my wife and sons whose love I have enjoyed throughout.

Thank you all, love and God bless.

Freddie

Foreward

This book is an emotive account of how a super confident, clear thinking and positive man was emotionally and for some time physically destroyed.

"Read this when you have doubts and remember it was given to you with all my love."

SHATTERED IMAGE
The Life and Loves of a Broken Man

Chapter		Page
	Introduction	1
1	Reflections	3
2	Genesis	7
3	Icarus	18
4	Atlas	27
5	Poseidon	37
6	King Midas	46
7	Helen of Troy versus Bacchus	53
8	The Magic Isles	70
9	Samson and Delilah	80
10	Joie de Vivre	93
11	The Great Lexdeo	102
12	The Great God Caritas	106
13	The Fall of Atlas	114
14	The Fall of Atlantis	136
15	The Venus Betrayal and Life goes on	160
	Epilogue	167

Introduction

Shattered Image is a biography of a Midlands man, who began life in the fairly sheltered environment of a normal post war family. His family like many other families at this time were trying to establish a life for themselves in a society accustomed to war and rations.

Brought up in the shadow of an older brother, who achieves success by hard work, Freddie Jones finds himself, in his early life, constantly being compared to his older brother. Throughout most of his life Freddie finds himself trying to outdo his brother, albeit not always by fair means.

His establishment in the business world observes initially the friends he makes and the foes he forages in the field of finance. His development in the business world led him as so many others, to a commitment in the world of the Freemasons, his role as a Magistrate brings new insights into the "behind the scenes" life of the world of business, politics and the law of the land. He experiences the hypocrisy of both in his deepest hour of need.

Shattered Image is the tale of a man who finds himself enveloped in a cosmopolitan lifestyle, travelling throughout Europe and rubbing shoulders with renowned celebrities. Expanding his business leads him to local fame, fortune and for a short while a double life, as he finds himself embroiled in a passionate affair with his assistant. It is an affair of great proportions which nearly destroys him. His restless nature leads him to develop new skills, sports and a new lifestyle. Deep sea diving and learning to fly lead him on to new ventures, whilst at the same time firing a warning shot over his head, warning him that he is treading on dangerous ground. Pride comes before a fall he was warned in his youth. He was to find out just how pertinent this phrase was to be to him, because for Freddie Jones, the fall in his case was to prove almost fatal.

1

Reflections

He stood, looking at his once smooth reflection in the large, gilt framed mirror. He had this almost strange sensation. One of those sensations that send your mind spinning and your head reeling. That er-r-r feeling of déjà vu. That was it! You know the feeling "Been there. Seen it. Done it!" You're not sure when or where. Was it this life or another? His breath stopped short of his lungs, it came in infrequent, short, sharp blasts.

He pondered the change in his once good looks. He felt almost as if he was staring into one of those fun mirrors, the sort that provide the curves and wrinkles where you didn't know that you had them. It wasn't just his features that appeared distorted in the reflection; however, something in his eyes suggested that there was more than that, something he couldn't quite put his finger on, something that he knew was there, but he couldn't quite grasp.

Why was he so surprised by what the mirror reflected? The same comfortable, lavish furnishings surrounded him. In the large, panoramic windows, soft, warm, velvet curtains hung in beautiful pleats, just as they always had.

In the centre of the room, almost alone amongst the other furnishings, sat a huge, plush velvet chesterfield. Its curves reminiscent of the sleekness of a wild cat and as soft as down. It was one of those suites you sink slowly into, stretching out your limbs to its full length and then as you slouch into the corner, you feel your worries slip slowly away. Television, video and audio cabinets, large and austere, matched the surroundings. And what about that drinks cabinet – well that would most definitely have required the number of Alcoholics Anonymous. To remove one bottle from the cabinet would have observed its collapse into a fit of the D.T.'s. He returned to the gold framed mirror, reflecting on a new man and he turned to reflect on a former way of life, a life he couldn't forget – his life.

His early days as a young child, even as a hot-headed youth had been so very different from what he had experienced since his stable and respectable marriage. He paused for thought. Funnily enough .... it wasn't his marriage that had made the difference. In fact, if anything ....there was one thing that had not changed, that was his marriage.

He glanced silently across at Gabrielle – at her calm, kind face. She was busy in her usual task of mothering the two boys. She still had that girl next door look. You know the type – peachy complexion, dark, natural wavy hair and eyes so sympathetic, so blue, so deep, they reminded him of the sea off the Greek Islands. His wife was one of those rare facets in life. He could not think of another who could fall so aptly into the category he placed her in – that of an angel. Her name was more than appropriate.

There had been times as Freddie lay motionless in his hospital bed, when he believed that he saw her silken wings and the shadow of a halo hanging in a mist around her shoulders. If he were to be of a superstitious nature

Freddie could have thought she had come from on high to save him.

Isn't that what she'd done? Saved him? But saved him from who or what? He was inclined to think, she had been sent to save him from his own self-destruction.

She had always been there for him and for the boys – mother, wife, nurse, decorator, teacher, even at times, in the early days a secretary. Oh God! The thoughts bounded through his mind. That word "Secretary" conjured up memories he'd rather forget, but couldn't.

The boys had always been there too, looking to him for support, for guidance, for example, for fatherly love and for friendship. Had he been that to them – a friend? Funnily enough, the one thing he had come around to in his warm, safe hospital bed, was the sweet smell of Gabrielle's perfume and the sound of shrill, raucous laughter from Paul and Danny. Danny was the youngest, his favourite – always bright, alert and full of laughter. Danny, with his usual sick sense of humour was telling a joke.

"Have you heard the one about the Irish Grandfather?"

He asked Paul.

"The Grandfather had just died, despite receiving a pace maker and was being buried. Suddenly, out of the blue, (or should one say, out of the sky), a bolt of lightning struck. The funeral party scattered, thinking they were being attacked by the IRA, as both Grandfather and pacemaker exploded. Talk about the funeral party being scattered, instead of burying Grandfather, they were able to scatter his ashes."

Both Danny and Paul burst into laughter, with Gabrielle shushing them for the sake of respectability and a thought for the other patients around. He was sure it was at this point, that he had awoken from his long sleep. He had certainly felt the well of laughter rising in his chest, although no sound, he was sure, could be heard. He couldn't be sure that this is what had woken him. He had been asleep so long, he had missed so much. But just what had he missed?

2

Genesis

He had been born at the beginning of the rising and prosperous fifties. Well, prosperous in comparison to a war torn Britain of five or six years previous, when buildings and families had both been torn apart. His parents, just like many other people at this time, took advantage of the growth in the service industry.

His father was from a family that had once been both prosperous and traditionally Jewish. Prior to the war, he had worked primarily, as an assistant to the General Manager, of a manufacturing company in the Midlands. His mother was from a large, hard working but less wealthy family, of no particular denomination. However, her skills, like those of most women, had been more practical. She had worked for a bakery and in fact she had always been considered a good cook and would be remembered for the aroma arising from the kitchen.

However, just like most women, his mother had known how to rise above her station; in fact she was particularly at home at this time when social mobility was the norm. She had known quite well, how to provide for her family, even when times were particularly hard. Food still appeared in plentiful supply on the table. He could never remember going without, even his pocket money was there as regular as clockwork.

Not that money or position had mattered to anyone in the forties and early fifties. In war torn Britain, all that had mattered was survival and after that the job of picking up the pieces, with or without your family and friends.

His father and his mother, had in fact met, just as many couples had at this time, in the course of their contribution to the war effort. Met! To say they met, was an understatement really. It was more like being thrown together, like two different strains of fish – a trout and a salmon – being caught in the same net.

They'd never really talked about their time during the war and he had never tried to push it, he felt the pain might have been too great – he did have some feelings. However, he was aware that his father had been a sergeant in the Royal Warwickshire's, but had never seen active duty abroad, due to his delicate situation with rheumatic fever. His mother on the other hand had joined the Women's Royal Army and had been seconded to radar, where she used to scan and watch the radar screens.

His parents had continued however, to go through rough times and they had actually succeeded, despite the usual setbacks and lack of family support. You see the marriage of his mother and his father wasn't actually Kosher. It had not been viewed by either family as something to be particularly well blessed. What a mixed marriage? Outrageous! They might just as well have married aliens. But what did his parents care about family or even outsiders' views, they were in love and thrown together by circumstances. They had fallen for each other hook, line and sinker.

Luxuries hadn't always been plentiful, but hard work and good fortune, had meant that they continued to move slowly, but surely, up the social ladder. They became more and more socially acceptable and as they did so, they moved to increasingly more prosperous areas, from a small nineteenth century terraced house in the middle of the Black Country, to a larger and more luxurious detached house in a quiet, hamlet, on the outskirts of the Midlands. Eventually, as their marriage blossomed, even the "Mod cons" or gadgets became more apparent and after a while of course, they were taken for granted, just as they were in many families.

His parents' happy contentment was crowned with the one thing that was sure to unite them or two things in this case! First, his brother had arrived to provide the cornerstone to the marriage, and then six years later, his birth had put the final touches and had consecrated and blessed the marriage. What did it matter if their families didn't bless them, they were on the whole a happy, small, nuclear family.

Perhaps, it was the fact that he had been born at a time, when people were still being exceptionally careful, particularly his parents. Or perhaps it was because everything was becoming more plentiful, including opportunities, that as he grew into a youth and into his adolescence, he tended to act as if everything was gilt framed. There for the taking! He knew, even at an early age, that he would physically reach out and grab every chance that came his way. Just like a tramp finding the price of a cup of tea on the pavement, or like the dieter in a shop full of cream cakes, he could not resist any temptation that was set before his eyes.

His problem, he knew, would be establishing himself in everyone else's eyes. At home, his brother, older than he, succeeded in everything he did – the apple of his parents' eyes. At the Grammar School they had both attended, it was his brother who had achieved excellent grades and it was his brother who knew what the future would hold for him. Christ, there were times when he wanted to shout, to make people notice him for himself. How could he break out of his brother's mould? How could he stop himself being looked upon as, the brother of........?

Because his brother had excelled in everything he did, because his brother had been trustworthy, they, everyone that is, had assumed that HE would be a reflection of his brother. He became Head Boy, just as his brother had; he was given responsibility, just like his brother. He felt himself running down the same track, his brother at the front, laying down the tarmac and making good, but try as he would, he kept getting caught in the dust that was kicked up. On reflection, it had been mostly his own fault – you see, he just couldn't resist flaunting the responsible positions he held.

He thought back to the times when as a prefect, he had allowed himself to be bribed by other pupils – not because he was gullible or easily influenced, but because he would get something out of it. They would bribe him just so that they could shelter out of the pouring rain. He thought of the times when he had given out punishments to pupils, whilst he was Head Boy, generally for some small misdemeanour, but maybe, even if, he was feeling a little mean that day. He would give them the task of picking up all the wrappers dropped and then return the wrappers to him. In the eyes of all concerned, he appeared the moral pupil, keeping the school litter free and providing a very fitting punishment to erring pupils. What they failed to realise was that by returning the wrappers to the manufacturer, he would be able to claim a camera, or some other much sought after gadget. He didn't need them. He'd already received many of these wondrous freebies from the manufacturers. What did he want with them? Well, of course, he was making a substantial profit by selling them to poor, unsuspecting gullible pupils. This was his first attempt at being a Salesman and a con artist, if ever there was one.

He had learnt from an early age, that it was necessary to con your way through life. But at the age of fourteen his parents had decided to move from their comfortable middle class home in the straits of Dudley, to a more prestigious detached property in the quiet hamlet of Heathton, near Claverley. Where he had been accepted in his old neighbourhood with a broad, "Faggots an' Pais" Black Country accent, now he realised that to survive in his new surroundings, he must adapt. He didn't find it too difficult to learn to speak smoothly, to adopt a sleek, strawberries and cream accent. However, he realised quite early that most of the residents of the village, were actually trend-setters who had also moved into the area and not the wise, old men of the village, as he had at first assumed.

He settled into his new home, the White House, at Heathton, quite readily – in fact his ego got quite a boost from living there. Can you imagine, being asked by some bountiful blond where you lived and with a modified American drawl, your reply would be "Well-l of course, I live in the White House", what more can one say!

The White House was in fact immense, compared to what he had been used to previously. The White House had a large, detached double garage and its pool!!! What? Pool? Oh sorry, I didn't mean to mislead you. It wasn't a swimming pool, more a sort of fishing pool really, but it was the only house in the area, as far as he knew, to have one at that time.

His time at his new grammar school, The Oldbury Wells Boys School at Bridgnorth, was just as riveting.

He threw himself into everything that was on offer, particularly if it meant having time off school, such as the three day jaunt to Eastleigh Barracks at Southampton. He was so captivated by the tours around the submarines and the warships; it was in fact surprising that he hadn't enrolled himself into the Navy. The discipline, he considered at the time, would have been too much for him to handle, however on reflection, some might say it would have done him some good.

At sixteen years of age, he joined the Duke of Edinburgh award scheme, with his outside activity being hill climbing and archery. The archery was a fantastic idea, or so it seemed in those days. At that age, imagination runs riot and you can picture almost anyone as your target, including the much maligned Headmaster. Hill climbing was great too; after all, it meant that he could miss Friday afternoon at school, heading for the mountains of Cadair Idris in Wales. The climb was a bit of a drag really, but he soon clocked onto the idea of popping into the local taverns and because of his size got away with the age problem. One very memorable night, he got really, truly silver awarded. His tent could have been in Timbuktu for all he had cared. In fact, by the time he had finished taking one step forwards and two steps back, it could quite well have been in the back of beyond. The nearest place to flake out had been a barn, where he pulled the bales of hay around him to form a warm, secluded straw coffin. He never really took to tents again after that.

Up to the age of sixteen, he had always smooth talked his way out of most situations and because of his up to now, supposedly good character, he was allowed to work in the metalwork room at lunchtimes and at breaks. The teachers were very impressed, particularly when he told them that he was making ornamental cannons out of aluminium bar.

Then one day the inevitable happened. He was pulled in quite unceremoniously, by the chemistry teacher, old "hairy" Harris. Mr Harris made it quite clear that he was aware of the real task in hand – that of producing crude gunpowder and aluminium shot. The worst of it was that he had also found out that it was being sold to the remedial forms and included superb firing cannons. Mr Harris went on to hold a demonstration of the capabilities of his manufactured product and the effects of his escapade, placing one of the cannons into a vice and setting the damn thing off. To this day there must be a crater in the Chemistry lab wall about two inches deep and two inches in diameter, where the aluminium shot lodged itself into the wall. Needless to say the aluminium cannon making facilities were withdrawn.

It was at this point in time that the school made him aware that they had sussed his ruse. They made it clear that he was not going to hit the heights so far as academic qualifications were concerned. They also made it clear that he did not show the same sense of responsibility that had been shown by his brother.

Still, he wasn't going to worry if certain activities were to be curtailed, was he? He'd just behave himself for a while; show himself to be the model pupil. Before long, they'd be putting the escapades down to "youthful spirit", "just one of those things", "a slip of character" – he'd soon have them eating out of his hand again. It was amazing, even at this age; he had this remarkable knack for the gift of the gab.

Have you heard the one about the Bishop and the young lady? Well, his next escapade involved just that. He was offered the opportunity to go on a thoughtful weekend; a religious retreat is what they called it.

"A fine chance for you to reflect upon your future. Who knows, perhaps you'll come back with a wealth of inspiration". His father had said.

His first reaction had been one of stupor. His father suggesting that He go on a thought provoking weekend. He, the master of thought! It could mean only one thing – boredom.

Still, off he trundled to Hereford. It didn't take a lot to convince him that he could have quite a good time, since his closest pals had decided they also would like a piece of retreating. It also meant of course, what they would be retreating from was parental watchfulness. By the end of the weekend however, it was impossible to say, quite who had done the retreating, apart from the Bishop of Hereford.

Their base was to be a huge, ancient farmhouse for the weekend and silence was the name of the game. Not much of a game I hear you say, well it's amazing just what you can do when it comes to "S-sh you know what!"

They spent the weekend in silence, nodding approval, or shaking their heads in denial – not that they had denied themselves all that much! On the final night, a rave was to be held, all vows of silence could be broken. Of course, the rave, as far as the organisers were concerned, involved soft drinks, low tempo pop music and a few plain crisps. He had far different ideas, as did his mates. Having found an adjoining, but secluded room, they promptly led the way for their young ladies. This room however, just happened to be the Bishop's study.

Oh! I'm sorry; did I forget to tell you? Yes of course there were females there too! What would have been the point in going if there wasn't! The love of his life was there, beautiful leggy Cherry. The one he had sworn his undying love to, well at least in sign language anyway. Cherry by the way, just happened to be her nickname, particularly after that night anyway.

To cut a long story short, he and his mates bunked off into this study, with their respective partners, to catch up on some of the er-r-r gossip they'd missed that weekend. All were in varying degrees of hectic conversation, when the door opened the light beamed on and in glided the Bishop, looking for all the world like some apparition. Unfortunately, or fortunately, depending on how you look at the situation, Cherry, his young lady had long, beautiful hair. Her hair hung way down past her waist and in fact it was only her hair which hid some of her embarrassment, when her hair got stuck in her zip, as he hurriedly tried to re-zip her.

The Bishop on the other hand, who had been, both a gentleman and a scholar, in his previous life, before taking a vow of celibacy, had obviously been in similar situations himself. With all the savoir faire he could muster, the Bishop reached on the shelf for the book he had apparently been looking for, switched off the light and drifted back out of the room as smoothly as he had drifted in – just as if it had been empty. Not that that made any difference to the situation, of course, the entrance of the Bishop had put a damper on the evening's activities for everyone involved. Apart from sheer embarrassment, they were all far too busy rolling about with laughter.

If fame or popularity, had not gone to his head by this time, then he felt fortune just might. His first chance at fortune came at a fairly early age, well in comparison to most anyway. As a youth, whilst still at school, he was offered the opportunity to become a Disc Jockey, well what can one say, except Tony Blackburn eat your heart out.

It all began really, as a bit of a lark. In the beginning

just something to fill in the dull moments. With any luck he could make a bit on the side and still have a laugh with the blokes. Of course, that dreaded problem of homework was bound to rear its ugly head, but this wasn't going to be a problem for him, was it? Hell no! You are joking. The lad that had such a great ability to worm his way through life, getting just what he wanted. In his usual, cunning, off-hand manner, he would manage to bribe someone to do his homework for him. Someone who probably owed him for a favour of some sort or other or some poor sucker who could easily be conned. It was a bit like being "The Godfather". Yeah, that was it and he quite fancied the title "Don" before his name.

As it happened, this DJ lark was a sure thing. With his suave, smooth good looks, he definitely got himself noticed and if anything it sure pulled the birds. Most of his friends were quite prepared to do his homework for him, for the icing on the cake – just a small piece of that fame and of course a share in the birds he managed to pull. If they were really, really lucky, they might even get the good looking one, just for the night.

Then of course there was the time of the successful television debut – well almost. He had auditioned for the part of Sandy Richardson in Crossroads. You remember, that old Brummie soap opera. He'd even actually got the part that was until; the powers that be had seen an abrupt end to this future lucrative career.

"Your path lies in another direction." He was told

"Silly, fairytale jobs on the television, in some soap opera are not for you." His Headmaster roared.

"It's time you pulled your socks up, got your head screwed on and started taking more responsibility for your future."

And, what could one do when the headmaster got the backing of your parents. Acting was not a reliable job, he had to stay on at the boy's Grammar School and make sure he completed his studies – just like his brother..................

His brother in fact, was making it big in engineering. Perhaps, he thought it wasn't such a bad idea, after all. His brother had his own furnished bachelor pad, his brother had a smart, fast car and his brother had a stream of the most beautiful women. In fact, he decided this might just be the time to follow in his brother's footsteps and he'd obviously please everyone. In fact with the sort of life his brother had, he'd even please himself too!

So, whilst still in the Sixth Form at school, he had a change of heart. With flying colours, he passed his driving test. With every enthusiasm, he purchased the neatest, fastest car, his present bank balance could possibly afford – a souped up Mini. Stirling Moss had nothing on him, not the way he used to drive that Mini – you'd think it was a formula one racing car. He made the car his future emblem for life – "turn the engine on, put your foot down to the floor and sod everyone else" – not even his spirit was left behind.

3

Icarus

Why had he stopped at this particular point in his life to reflect on his past? He had left the warmth and security of the hospital that he had grown to know as a second home. Was it the insecure feelings brought on by this departure? Was it the thought of leaving the crisp, clean hospital sheets and the security of the hospital bed? He knew he would be returning to them soon enough, too soon in fact, for more painful surgery. Those thoughts put off a return to the hospital. But while he was at the hospital, at least he felt secure. He felt a little like the ostrich hiding its head in the sand. While he was in hospital, no one, but no one could get at him to ask too many awkward questions. No press, no solicitors, no police. So why should these thoughts affect him? Why should these memories come flooding back?

Of course, the reflection in the mirror had revealed very little of his former self. In fact, if anything, he was almost unrecognisable. The point was that this change was not just in body, but in the strands of his soul also, almost as if he was searching for some sinister existence. The worry lines on his face resembled the deep grooves of tyre tracks, highlighting the wear and tear life had taken on him recently. His face belied a sad sunken smile and resembled a wreck awaiting salvage. The deep, distant eyes, they suggested a change to his deepest, innermost self. What had caused this change?

As a boy and as a man, he had held purely selfish ideals, thinking only of his own needs and desires. Now he held a much higher philosophy on life. He pursued both ideals and philosophy vigorously, treasuring life itself.

He sank slowly into the settee once more, pondering his innermost thoughts. He began once more, to scan the lines of his local rag. Of course! That was it! There on the very front of the local newspaper. A copy cat accident, similar to that of his own. A small, twin-engine plane had been brought down on the Welsh border by severe blizzard conditions. This time luck, or God, if there was one, had not been on the crews' side, only the co-pilot had survived.

He thought back to that fateful April day in 1988, the day that had changed his whole life. A life which had been rich and full. He had travelled to the small Midlands airbase through the local countryside. It was a beautiful sunny day, but one that was also crisp and cool. It was one of those days when the sun shone on the dew dropped fields and each blade of grass glistened in the fields around you, as if tinged with a little gold or silver leaf. Not that he appreciated either his surroundings or his fortune at this point in time. No, he was far too busy to appreciate nature, or the aces life had dealt him. Everyone had told him how fortunate he was, but things had happened far too fast, he'd taken so much of it for granted and well-l-l, he couldn't see then, what all the fuss had been about. But now, well now was a very, very different matter.

He thought back to that fateful day, when he had clambered aboard the small snow white, twin-engine plane. Even now he still got a buzz out of flying, whether he was a passenger or whether he had the opportunity to fly. It was the take off that generally triggered the senses, that's what sent all his senses soaring. The feeling that rises quite rapidly from the stomach, slowly passing into the chest. A little like blowing a balloon up, then suddenly and without warning, while you still have the balloon in your mouth, the air escapes and you gasp frantically for breath. The stomach, well that's left so empty that there's room for an aviary of swifts and in fact it feels like there is an aviary in there. It wasn't a feeling of fear, no, one couldn't call it that. No, more a feeling of excitement, than of fear.

He had prised the plane up gently, pulling on the wheel, with considerable ease. He was becoming accustomed to the controls on the flight deck. Being in the air, just like travelling, came as second nature to him these days. He had travelled the globe in recent years, always on the pretext of business – but always ensuring the possibility of a little pleasure too!

He had been lucky; his business had taken off, just like a plane into the clear blue sky. As a consequence, his life was more than just "in the fast lane". If he had to describe his life at this point in time, he would have said he was in the "air ways" above Europe. When he wasn't in the air learning to fly, he was down deep in the sea scuba diving, or purchasing a speedy, lavish new sports car. When he grew tired of one then he'd discard it, like last night's Chinese takeaway and he'd purchase another. Ferrari, Lamborghini, Maserati – you name it, he'd owned it. He loved the rich smell of the luscious leather seats, the neat gadgets – the stereo, the electric windows – he loved everything about the richness of these vehicles. They were his vehicles. Vehicles which said "Lookout Freddie Jones is about!" Most of all though, he got a kick out of the speed. He got this same kick when he flew a plane.

On that fateful day in April 1988, everything had seemed as it should be. There was nothing, not even instinct to suggest anything different. Of course, he had a very special reason for going, one which he was looking forward to, but which he could not disclose to anyone. The weather forecast indicated that it was a little cold, but otherwise a clear, fine, spring day. A few clouds here and there, but okay for takeoff.

They had taken on a full load of fuel, in order that they could complete their journey. He eased the plane up to a level just below the clouds; it was beautiful to look out over the landscape, for miles upon miles into a distance that seemed never ending. It felt almost like playing God. That's what his father had said at the time, only with a different intonation in his voice and with a different meaning than he would have given it himself. He could hear the Victorian, dominant monotones of his father's voice.

"If God had intended man to fly, he would have given him wings."

His father appeared to like these philosophical phrases. However, the saying he appeared to remember most these days, perhaps because it meant more to him now than it had then, was "pride comes before a fall." His father must have been a prophet of some sort; he couldn't possibly have known otherwise, the sort of fall he would experience. Perhaps he, Freddie, should have listened.

He handed over the controls to Ken, his air commander. Everything seemed to be going well, there was very little turbulence and the skies were quite clear. They'd been flying for about fifteen minutes when he began to get the feeling something was wrong. What was it? The look on Ken's face? The atmosphere? Instinct? Who could say?

"Problem Ken?" He queried.

"Something wrong with one of the engines" Ken muttered.

Suddenly and without any warning, the front screen began to frost over. Then as if to enhance their fears, the noise began – or was it a lack of noise? He couldn't quite remember now, what he had heard. But the engine was faltering. It had become iced up. The control gear wheel locked, the plane began to drop dramatically in height.

"Watch out Freddie!" Ken said "Something's wrong with the engine the carb's frozen up. We're falling. We're going down. Brace yourself. We're going to crash!"

Ken hurriedly put out the Mayday signal, giving their position. The funny thing is that in those few seconds, your whole life appears to flash before your very eyes, even though it seems like hours. Out of sheer fright, you think hurriedly. You try to think of ways to stop the inevitable happening. Then, just as quickly, you resolve to give in. At least it will be quick. A click of the finger. A blink of the eye. A word. And then. It's over. Just like that.

In those final moments, all he could think of was the boys. He wanted to ring them, to assure them that he hadn't suffered. He wanted so much, to tell them how much he loved them, something he'd done very little of and wished now he'd done a great deal more. He wanted to tell them to take care of themselves. To take care of their mother. If only he had a phone. Life is made of "If onlys!"

Then, as if in a power cut, everything went black. Nothing. He remembered nothing at all. Nothing that is, until he came back to consciousness, about three weeks later in the hospital. He had survived. But how he had survived, he would never know. His brother told him some time later, that he had actually died twice. Why? Why had he survived, against all the odds? Why him? He wasn't super human. His family had been told the worst right from the start, as soon as he arrived at hospital. He would definitely never walk again and even if he survived, well, it was more than likely he would be no more than a cabbage. That alone was like a death sentence, they knew that. For a man, who had been super fit, playing every sport he could master and living his life to the full – they knew he would not survive life in a wheelchair, or in a bed.

Perhaps something had happened to him, when he died in the hospital, which would give him the strength, not only to survive, but to return rebuilt, renewed. The second Bionic man. Perhaps all those years in the metal trade had paid off after all. One thing was certain, he realised he would not be alive, without the help of so many people.

He realised, as soon as his faculties returned that he certainly had to be grateful to the many that had made his survival possible. Later when he was to spend six months in a wheelchair, totally dependent on others, he would have time to reflect on just how lucky he had been and who he should really be grateful to.

Their plane had crashed into an extremely lonely, though beautiful area of countryside. An area that was just on the border of Shropshire. It couldn't have been more remote. The crisp, clear day, had quickly become a day that was dank and frozen so cold, that a silvery shadow hung over the entire countryside.

The farmers in the area had been tending their sheep. Strolling along in the absolute peace of the countryside, hunting guns slung over their shoulders, searching for the obvious signs of vermin, which might disturb their livelihood. The last thing they expected was to be caught up in some crisis. At first, they had glanced up into the distance. They remarked to each other about the large bird of prey which appeared to be heading in their direction. That was until, it flew directly overhead, over the brow of the hill and then – all they heard was the sound of an enormous crash. They felt the whole ground tremble – as if enduring an earthquake. The whole of the countryside in the direction of the crash seemed to fly up into the air.

As they raced to the scene, the farmers were in awe of the carnage that had struck what had once been a barren field. Wings, propeller and tail pieces everywhere. Was it possible, really possible that anyone could have lived through that? They quickly moved in, to see if by the remotest chance, there was anything they could do. Anyone they could save. To their utter amazement, both occupants were still alive. The pilot was babbling incoherently, but appeared less hurt than the other person in the plane. They used the word "person" tentatively, because they really couldn't tell whether this person was male or female. The damage done was so severe, the face was almost obliterated.

What should they do? Was that fumes they could smell? No matter, they agreed quite quickly that they really shouldn't move him, or her, unless it became imperative. You see, they had noticed just how low down his head and shoulders had become. They felt certain that his back was quite probably broken. No, they shouldn't move him. Not yet.

The farmers, in fact, were to play a double whammy that day. The one Freddie was later to become acquainted with, John Sankey, went off to his Land Rover to call the emergency services on his mobile phone. The farmers' quickness and that of the services, was to save his life. The ambulance arrived in a hail of sirens and flashing blue lights. Not that anyone would notice out there. However, the ambulance very quickly became bitterly, bogged down in the country mud. The farmers were to play their part again. Land Rovers to the rescue, a motor to tackle any terrain, they heaved to and pulled the ambulance clear of the mud.

He was to realise, although much later, that it was partly due to the farmers' foresight in not moving him and in their speed, that he was to survive. He also realised just how much, up to this point, he had taken the emergency services for granted. It was after all, due to the care and attention of the Medics and the ambulance men, that not only did he survive, but that one day, he would also be able to walk again.

Examining the scene, the Medics, were in fact in awe that anyone could still be alive. The dreadful injuries were just too difficult for anyone to perceive. He was told later, that on their arrival he was already blue from lack of oxygen. The Medics had detected quite quickly in fact, that he had at least two breaks in his back. They had to ensure as they removed him from the plane, they did not move his back, not one inch out of place. It had been like taking a splinter from the eye – one movement out of place and irretrievable damage could be done.

Both pilots were to be placed in the same ambulance. This provided the Medics with further problems. They were torn between two options, should they crawl along, in order to minimise further injury and yet risk him dying from loss of blood, before they even arrived at the hospital. Or, should they, risk possible death, through a seventy mile an hour race, over rough, shoddy, country roads, in order to get him to the hospital in time? They guessed all they had was approximately twenty minutes.

The Medics decided on the latter and with speeds of up to seventy to eighty miles an hour, Pete Old – one of the ambulance men, attempted to brace him all the way to the hospital in Shrewsbury, by leaning over him.

For the next three months he would take on a new role – that of a Frankenstein's monster. His body pieced together and wired up to numerous machines that would provide him with life. A new life. His "Angel" sitting silently by his side. She sat throughout, holding a cold clammy, deathlike hand, acknowledging the fact, that if he did pull through, he would never, ever be the same again.

4
Atlas

Life at work taught him to be a man of the world, in more ways than one. Career, car and emblem on the line, he began his working life as he meant to go on – speeding through life and learning by his mistakes.

His first job on leaving school, at the virginal age of seventeen, was with a fairly large national company, known as Aston Standard at Tipton in the West Midlands. Aston Standard were producers of metal. He began his training there, in departments he didn't even know existed – credit control, progress department, he even worked in the warehouse for a short while, no job was above or beneath him, he wanted to know everything about metal. He became close to the metal, carrying it about, he knew each piece intimately.

His love of travel began with the help of Aston Standard. Sent first to Banbury, to work around the extrusions at the aluminium mills. He learnt all the technical data, watching the process from the smelting down to the finished product. One month at Rogerstone in South Wales, to see the process of rolling aluminium sheet and plate, then homeward bound to Tipton to start training as a salesman. By the time he had finished, he was wedded to the metal truly, knowing its measurements by each inch, line and curve, internal valve and vein.

Now a saucepan is just a saucepan to most people. Aluminium saucepans, I hear you say, what a boring subject. However, it was aluminium saucepans which took the "Y" out of "yearn" for Freddie and gave him more metal than he would ever need to establish himself in business. Aluminium saucepans are made from nothing more than aluminium circles originally. But you have to use your imagination and Freddie did!

There was a rejected order of some five hundred pots. Well, not really what you would call pots just tubs without any handles on really. Now, our Freddie spied a nice little earner here, straight away. He contacted a company in Walsall and guess what, yes, you are right and they had five hundred handles he could buy.

These were pots which his company had consigned to the scrap heap. He saved them. He placed a handle on each and then he sold them off, for what in those days was the remarkable sum of five shillings each. Not something, which would make him a millionaire, not overnight anyway, but certainly gave him something, which took the lid off his life and gave him a handle on business deals. And so began his love of business and of money.

However, he wasn't always quite so smart. The company he worked for had a service area for the lorries. Petrol, diesel, all the facilities were available to the staff at a discount price. At the end of each month, the staff would settle their petrol account with the company. Taking his Mini into a bay to fill up with petrol one day, his head full of ideas for making more money, he proceeded to put four gallons of petrol into the tank of his Mini. Well, I should say – what he thought was petrol. Unfortunately, his car did not run too well on diesel and he got no more than a few yards down the road, when he realised what he had done. Alas, too late. His car chugged to a halt. What could he do? His only alternative was to dismantle the tube to the carburettor and pump out four gallons of diesel, down the drains and gutters in Tipton. Hence he had become known as Diesel Derek. Diesel for the obvious reason and Derek, well that's short for Frederic.

As a young man of the time, he was reasonably wealthy. Eight pounds a week from his job as a trainee salesman, a Mini car and life at a bungalow at Oak Croft in Wombourne, where his family had recently moved. He thought, like most young men of this tender age, that he was the bees' knees. In the Accounts Department, under the trainee supervision of one Heather Hackett, he was to learn a lot more, particularly about the opposite sex.

Heather was qualified and experienced, both as a Comptometer operator and as a female. About thirty years old, even now he could smell the musky, misty, heady perfume she wore. A dark and swarthy woman, she was very, very sensuous and he was to find out just how!

During the lunchtimes, Heather would lead him down to the local park. A small secluded park, that was just down the road from where they worked in Tipton. Sandwiches in hand, they trundled off on the pretext of discussing some training facility, more often than not, they returned sandwiches squashed but uneaten. Through the park, they'd hold hands and of course, they'd snatch the inevitable kiss. Wherever she led, even if it had been to the ends of the earth, he would have been prepared to follow. He was at a very gullible, easily influenced and virginal age.

The long awaited Christmas time finally arrived and as usual in those days of the sensational Sixties, a huge company party was to take place. It was to be held in Birmingham City Centre, in the night-club of a lavish hotel. However, not unsurprisingly, just before the party, Freddie, his car and a wall had a small disagreement. What could he do with his car off the road? Well, not to be outdone and even on eight pounds a week, he had to make a show. He hired a car especially for the occasion. After all, he intended to take the fair Heather to the Christmas Party. An attraction seemed to be developing between the two, even though Heather lived some distance away at Heath Hayes in Cannock. No distance was too far – not as far as she was concerned.

The booze flowed lavishly at the Christmas Party and awards were made throughout the evening for Salesman of the Year. They, Freddie and Heather, stayed close all evening. Of course, inevitably, the party was finally to come to an end late into the evening, or as some might say, early morning. As for Freddie and Heather, well-l the rest is left to your imagination.

Freddie built up quite a reputation, along with the skills and knowledge for knowing how to turn a quick buck. Throughout the following years of his career, he was to meet some notorious characters. The first of these was a man of particular concern known as Bill. Although Freddie knew where Bill worked, he frequently felt that the origin of his material was a little like a Chinese puzzle. The material always looked brand spanking new, but one couldn't always be sure of the ingredients. Freddie wasn't always sure where Bill got his material from. Lovely material, he had a taste for the good stuff and generally he was able to substantiate its authenticity, but that didn't mean anything, not when you knew your metal! That is how Bill got his nickname – "Burglar Bill" that is.

Further opportunities came his way to create wealth. Ipswich, to the uninitiated, may be an East Anglian town, but to those in the metal trade it refers to switching metal for money. You take your shiny, scrap – copper or aluminium, to the scrap boys and you get cash in return for it. Straight exchange – no receipts, no invoices – cash for trash one might say. Well our wide eyed boy, metal man, call him what you will, knew his metal and knew all the deals too.

One of the best deals he ever had was when he went into a scrap yard in Nuneaton. He bought some fire damaged stainless steel coil, which had actually been ripped out of a firm up north in Merseyside. He knew his metals all right did our Freddie. With great agility he proceeded to strip the coil down to the pure, virgin steel. Unblemished, unmarked by the fire, he cut it down into various widths. No one would recognise it, so he sold it. Who to? Well, he sold it back to the company who had sold it off originally as fire damaged stock. A substantial profit made – this was probably one of the best, nicest, tightest deals, he was ever to make in his early career, but it gave him an enormous taste for more. If he wasn't a millionaire at this point, then he was quite definitely on the right track. He was also very determined.

However, it was time he moved on, time to gather more experience in the outside world. He looked around for a position in the Aluminium and Stainless industry. A post was advertised in Oldbury, at a Stainless Steel and Aluminium stockholder, for a trainee sales representative. He applied for and was offered the post, at the substantial sum of sixteen pounds a week – a huge 100% increase on what he had currently been receiving. He tendered his resignation and as it was a huge company, people came and went all the time, no one would really miss him, no doubt even the fabulous Heather Hackett would move on to another. And so, he started work at the Pacific Metal Company Limited.

Here, at the Pacific Metal Company Limited, he stayed for what some might consider to be a lifetime – a lengthy twelve years from 1967 to 1979. They were vital years both for the country and for Freddie. Expansion and contraction were the name of the game. With the first sign of recession hitting the country by 1979, companies were cutting back or going into liquidation, rising unemployment had begun. For Freddie these were years of expansion, which were to continue still further, on past the first recession of 1979 and way past any other you may care to mention.

To say that Freddie expanded would be an understatement. It was from here that he was launched into the big time! Joining the company in 1967, he began as a trainee salesman and went from strength to strength. Inside Salesman, Sales Representative, Sales Office Manager, Sales Manager, General Manager and finally Associate Director – nothing or no one was to stand in his way. Just twelve years it took him to reach Associate Director. Perhaps reaching your goal too quickly makes you restless. You always look around for fresh challenges and he had certainly done that in the twelve ensuing years.

There comes a time in everyone's life when they start to get a little restless. Too long in one company, no matter what the size, or how successful you've been and you become bored, you become stagnant. His time was now. He wanted to find out what opportunities life held outside this company he had grown to know so well. He was ready for fresher fields, to chew the cud elsewhere. After all, he had been there for twelve years.

He travelled down to London to the company's Headquarters, to tell them that he was looking for pastures new. He spoke with the Company Secretary, Elaine Parkin, who worked closely with the Managing Director and was his close confidante – in more ways than one, if rumours were to be believed. He explained his needs to her over an extensive luncheon, in fact, the meeting with Elaine went on late into the afternoon. He obviously hadn't realised just how much the company valued his services, since the offer of a new car and a salary incentive to stay, came as a total surprise.

He got on well with Elaine. In fact, something began to tell him he was getting on more than just well with her. Whilst he knew how to make money and was a gifted salesman, he still had not as yet learned to gauge the female mind. With the evening getting closer, he commented to her,

"If we stay here any longer, we'll have to stay for dinner too."

"Well so what. If we stay here for dinner, who knows what might happen afterwards." Elaine purred.

She was definitely a woman of considerable experience and charm. But his experiences were limited as far as women were concerned and he still had a lot to learn. This mega wealthy, woman of the world, frightened the crap out of him. She must have done, for he cut the conversation short, although she was his superior at the time and high tailed it back up the motorway so fast that they dubbed him the knight of the laser table.

The next character to come along was to change Freddie's whole life – not once but twice. Whilst at the Pacific Metal Company, one of his biggest accounts was with GEC at Stafford. The Assistant Buyer there, one John Hammond, was capable of putting a lot of business Freddie's way. With the benefit of many, many, lunchtime dinners, sheepskin coats, golf bags and clubs

– John did just that!

Although Freddie wasn't aware at the time, this two faced man, was to become a partner in Freddie's very own company, Poseidon Alloys. He was to prove deceitful from the beginning and an absolute sham from start to finish. As far as Freddie was concerned now, he was a particularly obnoxious, greasy individual, who had an even more obnoxious wife. At approximately a height of 4'6" each they resembled nothing more than a pair of roadside trolls. A more repulsive couple he would never have the wish or the misfortune to meet again.

The voice of John Hammond at that time was like standing inside the tower of Big Ben, when it strikes the hour – booming and vibrating. A huge noise but very little action. Now, at this point in time, the name itself was like someone scratching their nails down a blackboard. He obviously saw Freddie coming. The wide eyed boy, trying to honestly make a fast buck. Well, I ask you, whoever heard of someone honestly making a million. John Hammond, the man who was to defraud Freddie of his dream and who would take his company, Freddie's very own company to the cleaners, for many thousands of pounds in one year to Freddie's knowledge. As far as Freddie knew it could even have been so very much more.

Freddie's company I hear you say. What company? With all the business deals going on between these two, particularly with Freddie's gift of the gab, John was soon suggesting to him that they start up in business together. He began by suggesting, then badgering and then nagging – night and day, he never let up. Freddie was justifiably frightened of starting up in business at this particular time. It wasn't a good time – 1979, the time of the first mini recession, businesses large and small were going into liquidation. The Midlands – "Home of Industry" was particularly badly hit, in fact it would be more correct to say that it was decimated. Abandoned office blocks, warehouses and factories stood like ghost towns after an epidemic of the plague. However, that wasn't the only problem for Freddie. He had by now married and he wanted to make sure things went without a hitch. Furthermore, his first son had recently been born; he didn't want to take any risks – not with his bride and new family.

However, the constant nagging finally wore Freddie down and he decided to investigate the possibility of setting up in a partnership with Hammond. Freddie certainly had all the customers he needed, many of his current customers would be more than happy to come over to him in whatever company he operated. But of course, you need finance and that in 1979 was not so easy to come by, money was not abundant and banks were a little hesitant about financing a new venture. However, they obviously liked his "wide eyed boy" appeal and viewed his idea and his finances well, since it didn't take much for them to make a decision.

The next item on the agenda was to find a suitable name for this company. Alpha UK, Alpha Stainless and Alpha Incorporated were all viewed as potential names. However, as far as Companies House was concerned, for registration purposes none of these were localised enough.

As it happened, Freddie had taken up a new sport, in which he had recently qualified. This new sport, a new interest for him, was that of diving. He had become completely engrossed in this sport. Why not call the company after something to do with the sport? Aqua metal perhaps? No, definitely not classy enough. Then the idea came to him. Why not call the company after the God of the sea – but which one Neptune or Poseidon? Well a holiday on the Greek Isles soon helped him to make that critical decision. Poseidon Alloys was created on the crest of a wave and swelled to enormous heights – that is before it was to come crashing down again.

5

Poseidon

Have you ever spent a short holiday near the coast in autumn? When all the crowds have returned home? When the air is silent apart from the birds, who are gathering, to take their vacation, in some distant, exotic, far off land? When the sun sets large and golden upon the distant horizon? And when the warm autumn breeze, leaves a golden glow, upon your face. I'm thinking of Wales in particular, though you may be reminded of some other distant, dreamy shore. Wherever it happens to be, you're aware of a sense of restlessness. A need to be! A need to do!

This was the feeling he had. The need to do! This need to be! He'd spent many years now working for the same company. He'd been married several years. He was successful in everything he did. The contented, happily married, businessman. But it was a little like a repeat performance of a popular soap opera – everything with rose coloured glasses. There was a need to do more, a lot more. His spirit was restless and as if the spirit of a siren was calling, he followed – not straight to the sea, but he was heading in that direction.

He needed to learn something exciting, something new. He needed to forget all about his daily pressures, develop new pressures. This of course was before his business venture with Hammond. Diving was to be the answer. He realised that initially it would be fairly boring. His initial training would take place in the local swimming baths. So, in fact, at first it would feel a little over pretentious. All dressed up in oil skins and nowhere to go. But once he got the hang of it, once he qualified there would be no stopping him. The world would be his oyster.

He was living in a small terraced house in Chapel Street, Wordsley at the time. His second marital home. It was a neighbour, Peter Judson, who first got him interested in diving. Peter Judson, the very confirmed bachelor, who set the curtains twitching - and why not? He had everything, particularly his freedom. Sunday mornings his diving gear would be thrown into the car and he would disappear for a couple of days. Freddie frequently listened, fascinated by Pete's underwater adventures. He felt sure it was something he could do.

Freddie joined the Dudley Dolphins – a British Sub Aqua Affiliated Diving Club. They held a full training course at Brierley Hill Swimming Baths, later he would have the opportunity of trying out the local reservoir and then onto the coast. But first the rigorous training. It was important obviously to be fit, to be able to swim fairly strongly. The training involved various exercises at the deep end of the pool, twelve to fifteen feet down picking up objects. You practice using the Aqua lung without the aid of the face mask at first, just to make sure that if you were under the sea you would still have the ability to breathe if your face mask accidentally became dislodged. Would you be able to breathe under water without the mask covering your nose and your eyes? He passed those exercises with flying colours – no problem!

Then it was on to larger things – a local reservoir. So what, I hear you say. What's so big about a reservoir?

Not a lot actually when you are on the surface, but when you try it deep down in the murky depths for the first time, it's pretty terrifying. There's no telling what you'll come across.

The first exercise was to practice first aid, to attempt to take back an injured diver across the reservoir. Unfortunately for our Freddie, he had to tow sixteen stone Peter Judson across the reservoir, not an easy task. Although he, Freddie that is, was fit, in comparison to Pete, he was a two stone weakling. Another exercise required Freddie to dive into the deep; this was to make sure that you could cope with the pressures which built up under the water. Obviously, the deeper you go the stronger the pressure becomes.

When you first take up any sport, most people would advise you to economise just in case you decide that the sport and you don't see eye to eye. Well, Freddie was no exception to this. He economised on various basic equipment, including the underwater torch. What the heck he thought, it's no different to an ordinary torch, just a few adaptations. In his case he adapted the area around the lens circumference, providing an extra lens with the use of flexible putty. Fine at first! But don't forget that pressure, it can play havoc with your necessities. Well you can imagine what it's like to be sixty feet down below the surface, when suddenly the pressure forces your light out. It just gave up the ghost and went out. The only way in the darkness that you can tell the direction of the surface, is by feeling the direction of the air bubbles.

In his utter panic and to some degree, because of his dislike of the dark, Freddie tapped the torch several times to encourage it to play ball. It did! Great! Except for one thing. Obviously the light when it's in operation, keeps most things away, things which are usually used to the dark. With the light out these things had strayed a little out of their path and a little close to Freddie and when Freddie put the light back on, there to his utter amazement, within twelve inches of his face, was the largest Pike he had ever seen in his life. Who was more frightened, he wasn't sure, but both darted off in different directions to the surface. In future, Freddie vowed he would stick to the day dives, allowing the natural light to penetrate the water.

After obtaining the required qualifications, he was invited to go on a day dive to Llyn Padearn near Llanberis in North Wales. A beautiful but desolate area. It was a particularly cold day and the surface was ice covered, introducing Freddie for the first time to ice diving. It was all quite logical really, but on his first journey through the ice, he was fascinated to be involved in breaking through, then throwing down a line through the hole. The point was that if you should want to resurface at any time, then you would retrace the rope so that you could find the hole made in the ice.

Since water is not generally of body temperature, it can obviously be a shock to the system at times when you dive into water which is icy cold. Our man from Atlantis didn't take too long to learn a trick or two. The first was that of filling his diving suit with water in order to combine the two temperatures. Can you imagine though, what it is like when you dive into ice cold water – to say the least, it's definitely a shock to the system and requires a sharp intake of breath? The trick here of course is to have a hot water bottle to fill your suit, thus easing the body temperature to the correct level.

Having taken the icy plunge, FJ torpedo thin, was followed by the overlarge Pete and the rope to the murky depths of the bottom of the lake. The shimmer of the mud released a mist as their feet sank into its body. The rest of the crew followed precariously behind. They hesitated. Each one stopped. Bodies curved to form question marks, each pointing towards the bottom. There lay shadows of a different nature. Closer, closer they swam. As they approached, they observed what could only be described as swag bags. That's exactly what they looked like. That's exactly what they were.

Each member of the crew took a sack and hauled it to the surface. Inside each sack they found a gloriously rich hoard. Silverware galore. Silver teapots, silver salvers, cream jugs – each one solid silver, inscribed with a crest. Each item taken in a robbery from a local mansion house some ten years earlier and thrown with disregard into the lake. Some six months later the whole crew shared out the loot, since it was never claimed by the house to which it belonged. It appeared that the owners couldn't recognise it, or was it merely that the owners had claimed far more on the insurance for the items than they were actually worth.

The major crime of a diver is to dive alone; it's something you must never do. Still our daring God of the Sea couldn't resist the temptation, couldn't resist the freedom of the waves. Holidaying with the family in South Wales, he took to diving forty feet down in Aberaeron Harbour. The freedom he felt made him happy and oblivious to the danger that threatened. Gabrielle watched anxiously awaiting his return to the surface.

Deep down in the swirling depths of the sea, currents pulling in different directions, Freddie was in trouble. He was gasping for breath, for some reason his air supply was malfunctioning and his emergency air supply, from the adjustable buoyancy life jacket had also seized up. Breathlessness from fear is one thing, this was something else. Something he had to cope with. The one thing he remembered from his training was that the life jacket, when triggered, would immediately inflate you to the surface. The one problem was that the pressure from the atmosphere increases the further down you go. The pressure of atmosphere on the surface equals thirty three pounds per square inch and for every fifteen feet further down you go, it is another half an atmosphere of pressure.

What was it he had been taught to do? That was it! You must remember to exhale the air from your lungs as you rocket to the surface, or else risk your lungs expanding to such an extent that in actual fact your lungs could burst. The air from your lungs seeps into the chest cavity, creating an embolism. It was at this point that Freddie decided to give up diving, since he felt that this was a warning for the future.

The adventure had been pushed to the hilt. He had enjoyed himself beyond belief, now it was time to give up. After all, he had his memories. Like the time he dived off the coast of Greece amid the treasures of lost civilisations. Diving in fact, with none other, than the international celebrity Jacques Cousteau.

After diving for just four or five years, he had travelled to Greece with Gabrielle. He remembered it so well in fact, because they had stayed in a horrendous hotel right at the end of the runway.

A visit to the pretty town of Piraeus brought about a chance meeting with the well known television personality. His large, though not austere boat, The Calypso, bobbed quietly up and down in the harbour. Everyone in the local town knew who this untidy looking boat belonged to. Jacques Cousteau was a regular to the local inhabitants.

Freddie had already made his decision to go diving off the harbour of the sleepy little town. Seeing Jacques boat just altered the exact location a little. Solemnly, though quite plainly guarded, Jacques' boat displayed strictly no admittance signs in several languages. This did not perturb Freddie. Our man of fine words was not one to be put off under any circumstances. He strode; no paraded would be a better word ...... right up the gang plank clutching his qualification book. Freddie's divers' certificate was thrust under the nose of the guard on duty.

The guard disappeared into the jowls of the boat, to speak to the person who remained in charge in Jacques absence – since he was not on board. Freddie would have pleaded, he would have begged – but neither of these words was in his vocabulary. Instead he did what he was good at. He used every ounce of blarney that he could muster, selling his ability to the men involved. It took a lot of blarney, for they did not suffer fools gladly. He explained his desire to look for ancient artefacts. He demonstrated his great knowledge of ancient artefacts, with overblown explanations. They weren't to know that the explanations given by Freddie were those of the only artefacts he knew and they had been read from the local museum booklet over breakfast that morning. Finally, an agreement was struck. He could accompany them the next day, on condition that he observed closely and touched nothing, unless of course he was called upon to give assistance.

It's peculiar, the saying is right – "Never judge a book by its cover", in this case he realised that he shouldn't have taken the boat on first impressions. What had at first appeared outwardly to be an old tub was very different from the inside. On closer inspection, there was a wealth of highly technical equipment to cover the extensive operations that they carried out, including sonar.

It began just as every day had begun, since they had arrived in Greece, crystal clear blue skies and scorching hot weather. The co-ordinates for the day having been provided by the coast guards, they set off to their place of anchorage. Everyone got ready to dive, the Calypso crew's suits were well worn and they were torn showing signs of the protection that they had obviously given the divers against the coral reefs. Of course, Freddie had to dive in style - a superb diving suit which stood out amongst everyone else's and his diving equipment, well that put everyone else's to shame. On reflection now, his suit obviously made it clear to all concerned, that he really hadn't done that much diving – not in comparison to his colleagues on this journey.

The dive itself was fabulous. The beautiful clear blue sea, off the Greek coast needs no bragging. The clarity allows you to observe water life that you would not possibly see anywhere else. A beautiful and tranquil day, rays of sunshine cascaded through layers of sea, highlighting the white of the sand beneath. The warm ambient temperatures of the sea created an extreme weightlessness, which you would find it difficult to imagine. Squids and coral beyond belief and fish of the most exquisite colours swam before them or clung to their sides.

Most of the artefacts that day were mosaics, inspired by the amount of land which had been pillaged over the centuries by the sea. The Aegean Sea. A sea which acquired its name from the mythical King Aegeais who had thrown himself into the water off a cliff.

It was a sad, sad story of a young man, the King's son, who had travelled afar to kill the wicked Minotaur, who had threatened their kingdom; if the son succeeded he was to return with a white sail billowing in the breeze. A black sail if he did not. As most happy tales go, he succeeded. He had actually killed the Minotaur. But this is where the tale turns sour, for so overjoyed was he with his victory that he forgot to change the sail and he returned with his black sail still flying. Seeing this, his father thinking his son to be dead, threw himself off the cliff at St Michael's Mount. A mount upon which a temple was built and upon which a chapel stands to this day.

Jacques's crew had been more than receptive. They were exceptionally hospitable and invited him to attend a final drink at the end of the day. He waited anxiously in anticipation, hoping he would be invited to attend as an extra crew member aboard the Calypso during the rest of his stay in Greece.

But they must have guessed that his fascination was with glory and not with artefacts.

6

King Midas

From King of the Sea to King of Manufacturing and Sales. It seemed that whatever he touched turned to ....well, if not gold, then certainly money, in those early days.

Poseidon Alloys Limited was born, though not created in 1979. Bearing in mind that at this initial stage the partners had no premises, no material, no equipment, no money, nothing! Undeterred the pair set about fitting out the loft of Freddie's house in Chapel Street, Wordsley. With the aid of an electric typewriter and some printed letterheads, they proceeded with business providing invoices to their customers on their "designer" headed paper, selling metal on a day to day basis. Bearing in mind, that at this time the day job at Pacific was continuing, all the deals that had to be done, all the paperwork that had to be completed, all had to be undertaken at night time.

So, he finished one job at five or even six o'clock at night and then travelled into his loft, working for the best part of another three, four or even five hours, typing and arranging deliveries for the next day and so on. This went on for approximately six or seven months, in the summer being cooked alive in the loft and in the winter freezing to death, whatever the temperature, it proved quite a success.

Transport was little problem, since they already had

valuable contacts through their current line of work. Using initially, outside carriers, until the time when they felt able to purchase a second hand lorry and to employ a driver. This driver was none other than Gabrielle's father, Jim Dangerfield. With ever increasing orders, Poseidon rode the wave of the mini recession and grew to an uncertain height.

At this point, it was realised that their pool of contacts and business acquaintances had outgrown their present facilities. A new and larger harbour must be discovered, if they were to expand and swell with the current flow and cater for the ever increasing ocean of customers. Suitable offices and a warehouse were discovered not too far away in Amblecote. It was at this point, with the lease officially signed, that in reality Poseidon Alloys was officially and commercially launched.

The whole idea of the company was that Freddie, he with the gift of the gab, would undertake the purchasing and the selling, after all that's where his contacts lay. John Hammond on the other hand, agreed to handle the money and finance side of things – wasn't he on to a good thing!

Bearing in mind that Freddie and John had had the best of both worlds previous to their own business launch, an excellent job in the daytime, with company cars, expense accounts and also making money from their own company in the evenings.

Money was arriving from all directions. Although of course, prior to finding their own premises, they were taking nothing officially from their own business, but allowing it to float back in, in order to build on its strength. Of course, it depended on them keeping the whole matter particularly quiet, since their respective employers would have been none too impressed had they realised that their employees were in fact buying and selling on their own behalf. However, they should have known better, keeping information about success and keeping their own names anonymous was hoping for miracles. News of their successful trading spread like molten metal.

It had to happen! The fateful day arrived. A telephone call from the Head Office in London. They had had reports that he was carrying an interest in another company. They were coming up to see him. In fact, so serious did they consider the matter that they would be seeing him the very next day.

They had rumbled his tactics; they had sussed his activities – albeit in his own time, your own time does not exist, not when you are contracted to an organisation. It was like a marriage and they felt the cheated partner.

The same grilling was to befall Hammond, although his fate was a little more cooked and fried. They saw him. They grilled him. He said nothing. They dismissed him. No excuses accepted. Just goodbye. With Freddie it went a little further. They investigated, they checked and double checked. They felt deceived and felt he had gained an advantage through his deception. Of course, as far as their companies were concerned, there was every possibility that John and Freddie had poached customers and this would have been taboo and had to be investigated.

Then the worst happened. The commercial division of the fraud squad in Birmingham investigated the affair. The investigation continued for some six or seven months. The fraud squad drew a blank. No corroborative evidence of a deception could be ascertained. They dropped the case. The whole of the Stourbridge area could have heard the sigh of relief from him and of course his family, not to mention John Hammond. Needless to say, the orders from GEC Stafford ceased, with the demise of John as their Assistant Buyer, but Freddie could easily make up the losses, particularly now that he was giving full attention to Poseidon.

The new warehouse wasn't the best warehouse as far as structure was concerned. To start with the fork lift truck couldn't manoeuvre easily around the place. But beggars can't be choosers and it was a good start. They had office furniture – which they had purchased from various companies, many of whom had gone under in the recession. The next thing to acquire was a secretary or Girl Friday, who would be prepared to take the irate calls and make their excuses. To act as a receptionist, a Miss Moneypenny, a coffee percolator, general dogsbody and mother hen to two very busy and enthusiastic businessmen. They advertised the post, interviewing a variety of people and this is where Freddie's wife came in.

Gabrielle worked as a teacher in a local secondary school. She knew of a pupil, a young girl, who was trying to get a job in office work on leaving school. An enthusiastic and communicative young girl, known as Helen. An interview was arranged and she flew through it with flying colours. Well almost. As good as any school leaver could. Helen was very pleasant, mature and almost seventeen years old. Very confidant, a pleasant personality, nothing spectacular to rave about, but a rather engaging smile. She seemed a very capable young lady, able to undertake the work involved, able to sustain the jibes from two hardworking businessmen. She was taken on instantly. That was the basis of the company. John Hammond – accountant, bookkeeper and financial controller. Freddie - buyer, seller, stock controller and administrator. Helen – as described, general dogsbody and caffeine injector.

This was just a beginning. The start of an inspired company. The name itself, conceived by his love of diving at that time. They had everything going for them – they knew that they could make it, particularly with Freddie's knowledge of the trade. They felt certain that they were going to succeed. Poseidon in fact, became his mentor; it took over his life completely. It involved getting up in the early hours of the morning and slaving until late at night, seven days a week. He lived, breathed, ate and slept Poseidon. There was nothing else in his life, at this point in time, that meant quite so much. Freddie's wife, well she was there supporting him as usual, giving him encouragement, acting mother and father to his child.

Freddie's flying career almost began a little earlier than planned. They had had a huge sign made for the outside of the building, just to let everyone know they were there. It had to be huge to represent the size Poseidon was to become, or so they felt at the time. The sign having been made up arrived on the windiest day of the year. But Freddie wasn't going to wait to hang it. No, it must go up instantly. He wanted POSEIDON in bright lights. Unfortunately for Freddie, whilst hanging it, a huge gust of wind almost carried him away on the back of the sign. Perhaps he should have taken this as a sign!

Maybe, it was an omen of things to come. But when you're riding on the crest of the wave, you don't necessarily see the seabed.

From the early days, he should have been more aware that trouble was brewing. His partner John Hammond had decided it was more in keeping with his status, as a director of his own company, to drive a Daimler

Sovereign XJ6, rather than the cautious Capri that he had chosen. His flashiness should have been a warning at this early stage. Having separate autonomy, enabling each to sign the cheques individually was also a mistake, but it's no good being wise in hindsight. For the first few years of any business, it is wise to plough as much of the money back in to stabilise your base. This had been discussed. But on reflection it was much of Freddie's share of the money that was being ploughed back.

On top of all this, John rarely if ever, used to arrive in the office before 10.30am in the morning. Generally speaking his day would be all but complete by 4.30pm, providing Hammond with a very short lived day and the life of Riley. However, since Freddie was hell bent on making this company succeed and was oblivious to everything else at that time, it never occurred to him that Hammond was swinging the lead, on the very back of his own efforts. Life was still being very good to both of them. Business was booming. They had a good circle of customers and a good reputation in the trade.

Freddie worked extremely hard, but he couldn't help but be curious about Hammond, who twice a month would secretly and mysteriously steal off to an unknown rendezvous. His effort in the company was minimal. And as the story progresses his true character shines through, it was amazing that with so little effort he managed to bring in any business at all. However, as their partnership developed, Freddie began to understand the reason why Hammond would vanish. He was provided with a brief explanation of these secret visits and in fact was finally invited to join the secret world of the Freemasons.

Two stories in fact emerge at this point in Freddie's life. The first, his introduction to the secret world of the

Freemasons. The second was something which was to alter, to shape and to change his life forever. Since John Hammond was so frequently away from the office and in fact did so little work when he was there, Helen became Freddie's "right arm". They were thrown together. She had an enormous sense of humour and knew how to make light of a situation when necessary. She knew how to take the pressure off Freddie when the going got tough. She developed a mature and easy personality. Easy, in the sense of easy to get on with. Jokes, jibes and teasing came naturally between the pair. The chemistry began to work. The electricity began to flow, sparks flew. A relationship was beginning to take shape.

7

Helen of Troy versus Bacchus

Given the close proximity in an office so small, it was no wonder that their relationship took off as it did; in fact, it was a little surprising it hadn't got off the ground earlier. The usual poking and prodding, the usual jokes and jibes were a matter of course. All was undertaken, in a sort of brotherly and sisterly affection. The squeezing around the filing cabinets and each others' bodies was the obvious next step.

This one day was like any other light hearted day. Freddie crept quietly into the office up behind Helen and planted his hands on her waist to tickle her. Normally, she would have darted out of the way playfully, or perhaps hit him around the head with whatever she was holding in her hand. But on this occasion she spun around. Eye contact was made and the positive electrical charges were ignited. They stood, for what seemed like an absolute age, but what must have been only a couple of seconds. It was at this point that he realised that she was no longer the young cheerful, naive, school leaver he had taken on some time ago, but in fact she was now a young lady, with all the curves and bumps in the right places that this implied. In fact, she was a very well endowed young lady. Thinking about it now, it was funny he had never noticed this before.

As she spun around, his hands had been on her hips and were about to move to her waist for the usual tickle.

Her movement meant that his hands had strayed that little bit further than he had originally intended. Igniting still further charges, he stopped himself – not suddenly for it seemed like an age and almost as if he was not the only person involved, but rather disjointed from his own body. He didn't want to spoil this special relationship they had built. But then again the force was almost too great; the urge was too great to fight. It was as if he had two voices inside his head, one telling him it was wrong to take advantage of the situation, the other egging him on, telling him to go ahead. Live for today, enjoy yourself! His hands dropped down dejected, the halo rose – for a second. She looked him gingerly straight in the eyes.

"Go on then!" She urged.

Stunned, he placed his thumbs teasingly underneath her top, just at the waist.

"Go on!" She whispered seductively again.

He slid both of his hands from her waist slowly upwards, then around the front where her womanly curves arose. The mounts were like twin mounts of Vesuvius, huge, smooth and fiery. There was definitely something there waiting to erupt and he, felt the need to be there when the eruption took place. He wanted to be there waiting, when the lava fiercely flowed over.

Their eyes met. Their lips like magnets were drawn together. An incredible, mind blowing, electrifying, stunning kiss. It was like a freeze frame. The world had stopped in time. He had never experienced anything quite like this before. He was a married man. A man of the world. Reflecting now, it quite probably was lust. It was definitely fun. But it developed into what can only be described as the most incredible love affair and relationship ever to happen. He was torn two ways.

His thoughts at the time suggested that it couldn't go on. Someone was going to get hurt. How right he was! Little did he realise at that time, that so many years later, after so much had passed between them, that presumably both of them, would be devastatingly hurt.

Very little else was said for the rest of the day. They went home, each to their own respective homes. The next day everything seemed to be back to normal. A bright and cheerful day, he arranged to have lunch with her at a pub on Kinver Edge. An appearance of normality reigned. An "appearance" for that was all it was, just an appearance, could not be left as it was. The lunch was arranged to discuss the various problems that would arise, if they continued going in the direction, they had started the previous day. This lunch was arranged for them to discuss their feelings for one another and how they would cope with working together in such close proximity.

It was meant to set the stage. To throw light on the situation. Their feelings for one another were, or had been up to the present, purely an aspect of fun, of joviality, of laughter – nothing more than that. Although by now, the thought of lust had crossed his mind. He was finding it difficult to keep his eyes off her. For that matter he was finding it difficult to keep his hands off her. Her heady perfume mixed with his emotions. Her laughter, her smile sent a tingling feeling throughout his body. He couldn't remember the last time that he had felt this way. In fact, he couldn't remember ever feeling like this.

A quaint, quiet old world pub was chosen which provided excellent, sumptuous meals. A respectable, secluded pub, which would allow them to discuss their problems discreetly. They sat quite close together, their heads bowed, nibbling at their lunch. He was lost in thought, wishing that the slender chicken leg he found so succulent, was actually her leg, the small new potatoes, her ear lobes. When lunch was over, they sat even closer together, heads bowed in conversation. They discussed themselves. They discussed the people who would get hurt. What of his wife? What of his child? What of her boyfriend?

Freddie was amazed to discover that a part of this lover's tryst was due to her current boyfriend, who was later to become her husband. She had discussed with her boyfriend how well she got on with her boss; he had not hesitated in suggesting to her, that she try it on with her boss – just to see what would happen.

How far would he, Freddie go? What would it be like? How would the two – boss and boyfriend compare? However, this was not to suggest that she did not have ideas of her very own.

Freddie reiterated his comments to her. The fact that one or both of them would get hurt if they carried on. Subdued in thought they decided to go for a walk along Kinver Edge. First of all quietly side by side, each in their own thoughts, rapt in each other's presence Then slowly, as they walked, almost naturally their hands touched and came together, a spark of electricity was ignited. Side by side, hand in hand, on a beautiful sunny, spring day.

They stopped. Almost as if drawn by magnetism, their eyes moved slowly to make contact. Then their lips, drawn together, soldered into place, they made a kiss of bliss. The inevitable was of course to happen. Legs unable to stand the enormous strain, feeling like leaden weights, they gave way in a moment of passion. There in the middle of nowhere, they slid to the ground, still clinging to each other passionately and then inevitably they found themselves lying together, there in the middle of a field, encouraged by the rays of an early sun.

He leaned across her rather ample, but scantily clad body. Encouraged by her warmth, encouraged by her smile, by her eyes, but also encouraged by the sound of her intermittent heavy breathing, they kissed again. They looked at each other searchingly and then they kissed again. Not a short peck of thanks or one of greeting, but a hot lingering, passionate kiss which said that they were hungry for more.

In the hot passion of the moment, in the writhing of their bodies, her skirt began to rise. Or, was it he himself, who had edged the skirt further up? He couldn't remember now. As the skirt rose, first to her thighs and then slowly, so slowly crept to her hips, he caught a glimpse of what could only be described as the most beautiful pair of satin, mauve coloured, lace edged French knickers. They fitted her body so beautifully, so naturally, they were like a second skin. They felt beautifully soft, beautifully exciting. He wanted more, much more. It was obvious they were not going to stay in place and she made it clear she had no objection. Slowly, so slowly they were removed in a motion of timelessness, sliding down with ease, revealing beneath her smooth skin. He had to touch, to feel, to make sure that they weren't one and the same, to make sure she was for real. He marvelled at the silky smoothness, at the great sensitivity of her skin. As the satin knickers slid down they revealed the wide but slender hips she possessed, they revealed an area of beauty, of soft gentle curves, of warmness. He was lost, lost forever.........

Not used to sowing his oats elsewhere, but having been happily married, or so he thought up until that particular time, none of this came naturally to him. He fumbled. He fought with his conscience. But more than anything he fought with himself to contain his passion. His particular prowess on this occasion, due to his inexperience in this area, would probably he felt at the time, only have earned him a possible three out of ten, if she was asked to score him on his ability and sensitivity. It was all over so quickly. Not exactly an awe inspiring moment he felt, particularly for Helen. However, if Helen was out to get him, then she had already built her Trojan horse, she had led it to the gates; she had teased the enemy and offered the goodies. Now she awaited her glory.

Being a little flushed, they tidied themselves up. They made their way back to the car and drove back to work. It was inevitable that the change in atmosphere would be felt. John Hammond shot a few enquiring glances in their direction. Although he knew they were having fun together, he thought that their good relationship was purely on a business level. He was not to know that this in itself was the start of a truly wonderful, incredible love affair. Helen was undeterred by Freddie's initial clumsiness. From that moment in time, it was clear to both of them, clear to himself and clear to Helen, that this wasn't just sex, it wasn't just about having fun, it was everything. This was serious.

This was the start of a love affair, the sort you only read about in romantic novels. The kind of love affair which means everything, everything in the world. His need for her would be everything. He was to become obsessed with her to the limit. She was to become an all consuming passion. It would be a destructive love affair, where one or both would be destroyed, however, neither he nor Helen could see this at the time. Their love for each other became far too great, so great they thought that it could, if need be, weather any storm. They could, they felt, deflect any vindictive comments they might come up against.

The major difficulty of course wasn't in living with these feelings, but in having to hide them. He didn't want to hide them. He wanted to shout his passion, shout his love from the roof tops. It was like living a double life." The secret world of Freddie Jones". He was no longer under any misapprehension, if she went out of his life; he knew there would be a massive part of him missing. A huge void would exist in his life. It was all very apparent then, that she was going to become very, very important to him. She would become the hinge pin of his life, the steel drum he needed to beat, the length of metal coil he needed to wrap around himself. If the film industry had needed actors for the film "Fatal Attraction" then he and Helen would have fit the bill like a pair of kid gloves, it had almost certainly been just that - a fatal attraction.

After Helen and he had begun their romantic affair, an interlude which was to last some ten years, he became torn and tormented with guilt. Although, interlude is perhaps the wrong word to use, since it would suggest that it was sandwiched between two objects or phases. His guilt reemphasised the hurt that could be created for everyone, for Helen, for himself, for his wife, but especially for his child. Pure selfish thoughts also raced through his mind. Selfish arguments concerning the loss of his house, his company. His company, Poseidon, which had meant so much to him, it had been his life, his passion; it was the be all and end all. His home by this time was a rather large and austere house in Wombourne, with a double garage and a swimming pool. All this had been built using his own fair hands or his own hard earned money. He had a rather grandiose lifestyle at that moment. All this would be at risk. He could go wherever he wanted, do whatever he wanted and have whatever he wanted. Now it appeared he could also have whoever he wanted!

If the affair was going to go on, then the subterfuge would be great. He was going to have to be careful. He had worked so hard. He had worked all the hours needed to build up his beloved business. No one, but no one was going to take that away from him. If Gabrielle found out about his little sideline, then she would be entitled to ask for half of everything. It would literally mean ruin. He couldn't risk that, not now, not when he had come so far.

Success in his business had provided him with enormous confidence, not that he needed any in that area, his salesmanship was second to none. His success with Helen provided him with confidence in another area, the area of relationships, the area of love, an area in fact which he had not realised until now, that he lacked. But still he must keep things quiet; he could not risk the loss of his beloved Poseidon, no matter how much he loved Helen. He could say nothing until he was ready. It was like a game of chess, building a defensive line of pawns, ensuring support from the mighty authority of bishops and castles and then ensuring the safety of the kings and queens. All the pieces must be in place first and then he could put his cards on the table.

His whole life changed. He modelled himself on James Bond and in fact he even resembled him a little. He had developed a love of fast living, fast cars, expensive hotels, expensive meals and a love of dangerous sports. In fact his business was taking off so well, that he was spending more and more time away from home, setting up new business ventures around the country and even outside the country. In fact, if anything, his tremendous confidence began to make him a little arrogant. He began to want more and more, if he couldn't get his own way, then he would buy his own way. If people stood in his way, then he would charm them first and if that didn't work, he would buy them second. He intended to make the vehicle of life easy and well oiled. He knew what he wanted and no one was going to stand in his way,

Perhaps, in some ways his relationship with Helen had been a mistake, on reflection of course, because at the time he would have nothing said against her. But now, looking back, he could see he had allowed someone not only to get the better of him physically, but also emotionally. Mentally, he had been ruled over, his brain, his soul, his entire being had been taken over by another human being and then he had been torn apart – limb from limb, cell from cell. Every minute particle had been taken over by someone else. Whilst she was around, everything was fine, but it was a little like the story of Samson and Delilah, one day she would cut all his strength from his body In fact, she began to mean as much to him as his beloved Poseidon, one became very much entangled with the other. One day, however, the King of the Sea would be dragged to the seabed; he would be brought down by the current and savaged by the wailing Siren, never to resurface again. One day in the not too distant future.

He became as obsessed with Helen as he was with Poseidon. He wanted to know more, he wanted to know all there was about her. He wanted to know how her mind worked, he wanted to know everything she had to say, how she felt about a certain thing, certain people. He wanted to know about her family, her friends and most of all about her boyfriends – her former intimate relationships, what she did, where she went. The problem was that the more he knew, the more jealous he became. The more besotted he became, the more angry he became. He wanted to be the hunter; he wanted to be the one to place a mark in her life. Her current boyfriend, who was by most accounts, a fairly decent, hardworking, Black Country bloke, really didn't seem to be the sort for her. Some might dispute the accent on fairly decent, since he had originally encouraged her relationship with Freddie. But who knows what goes on in people's minds. Perhaps he had said it in jest. Freddie couldn't fault him. Since without the boyfriend's encouragement, Helen and he, Freddie, might never have come together. Still their private glances continued. The close proximity at work continued. Their warm, electric contact continued, although discreetly when at work.

Business at Poseidon was expanding tremendously and as already pointed out Freddie was travelling away more and more. As a consequence, his wife who saw less and less of him, noticed nothing out of the ordinary when he spent even more time away than was necessary. Helen and Freddie spent every moment together that they could possibly steal. The expanding business would provide even more opportunity. On one occasion, he was looking at the opportunity of gaining more business in the Newport area. He set upon the idea that Helen could go with him and suggested that she accompany him as his secretary for the day, since she was after all just that, his secretary.

The business meeting having gone exceedingly well, he came away feeling as inflated as a helium balloon. Helen and he went back into the town and stayed at the Black Lion Hotel, first for a bite to eat, then booking in for the day, for a little more food, this time for the food of love. Having had a delicious lunch, they made their way upstairs to their room. Making love to Helen was a totally new experience, one he had never come across before. It was the type of love making that started the violins playing, the drums banging, the stars bursting in the sky. This was true love.

Their love making was open, it was honest. They discussed everything and anything. They experimented with ideas that he never knew existed. He realised how restricted his life had been up until this moment. She discussed her present relationship with her boyfriend, how they made love and the fact that during their love making she had experienced four moments of bliss. Not to be deterred, Freddie with his new found confidence, could not let anyone get the better of him in anything, he had to drive the bargain home further, he had to go one better. The true salesman to the end. Inexperienced as he was, he was adamant that they were not going to leave the room that afternoon until she had reached her moment of bliss. He would make sure she experienced her fifth moment of bliss, her fifth orgasm.

The fact that Freddie was older than Helen made no difference. He had no reason to doubt his ability, his staying power. He was fit, disgustingly fit, because of all the sports that he played and the rigorous work out he put himself through quite regularly. It wasn't difficult for Helen either; it was a work of art for her. She was an artist in the true meaning of the word. Oblivious to the world around them, they realised their personal goal and reached the magic five that afternoon. He had beaten her boyfriend. Another case of one upmanship, a sense of achievement. This had been his goal, his target and he had realised it. It hadn't been easy this had taken its physical toll. Both were considerably relaxed. Both felt elated or even sedated might be a better choice of word

Tired and glowing, they dressed and went down slowly, enjoying each other's presence for the evening meal, before leaving and returning home. This was only the start; more extensive times together were to come – the overnight stops, the long weekends away, all these were to provide a future together, albeit short in comparison to some.

They drove back in silence, basking in the warmth and contentment that glowed from each other's body. Freddie dropped Helen off around the corner from her house, since they still did not want to attract any attention, the pretence was important to keep up. Suspicions were not to be aroused, not even with her family. Not for the time being, at any rate.

Arriving at his own house, his wife enquired about his day. Freddie a little on edge because of his deceit, jumped at her question. How did she know? What did she know? Then he calmed slightly, realising that this was the question she always asked. Steady, dependable Gabrielle. He informed her that he'd had a hard, but very successful day and smiled to himself. If only she knew how!

The next day he rose, went to work at his usual hour, about 7.30am, however there was a subtle difference that day. He felt considerably younger, although physically the worse for wear.

He walked uncomfortably, as though he had just clambered precariously off a horse. It felt literally as though someone had given him a severe kicking in his intimate area. The pain went on for the best part of two days. Was this the penalty? Was this the punishment for the illicit day in Newport? Was he to be put off? No way! He was more in love with Helen now than ever before.

His great Poseidon continued to go from strength to strength, building a reputation that was to be second to none. It was his Poseidon. He may have been in partnership, but he had built the company, one might almost say "with his own fair hands!" It was he, who had at first loaned his home to be a handling store, a warehouse, a telephone answering machine. He, who had worked all the hours required, until he was fit for dropping. IT, Poseidon was his. No one, as far as he was concerned was going to take Poseidon from him. It was his destiny in life to continue to go full speed ahead and take the company to its height. Who was going to stand in his way? Who indeed!

Noticing the discreet liaisons between Freddie and Helen and as if not to be outdone by what was going on, John Hammond decided in his own wisdom to taste the fruits of life as well. After all, why should he be left out of all the fun of the fair? Freddie noticed that John also began to turn up with a lady in tow.

Well-l-l lady was not quite the word that Freddie would have used, but he thought that if John was happy, well what the hell. Unbeknown to Freddie at the time, the constant outings to which John took his new lady friend the unlimited expensive lunches, the untold race meetings, all of these were paid for on the expense account of Poseidon.

Freddie would never have noticed, he was far too happy. No! Deliriously happy was a more appropriate term to use. After all, he had the best of both worlds, hadn't he? He had a thriving business, plenty of money, a wife at home, a mother at home to look after his children, to run the house and make everything nice and he had a mistress. Now you might consider him to be arrogant, you might say he was selfish, you might even say he was a male chauvinist, amongst many other things. However, Gabrielle he felt was treated well, after all didn't he work hard to provide for his wife, for his family.

They had everything they wanted. They had all the luxuries in life. He kept up the appearances of the good husband; he had no intention of embarrassing her. He felt his deceit was great enough without doing further damage. Anyway he bought her luxury cars. He worked hard, extremely hard – as far as everyone was concerned, he was the successful, devoted husband and father.

With Poseidon growing, he decided to take the business further; he would go all the way. He would expand his business interests abroad. Obviously, he realised that he would also need banking facilities abroad. He decided to look into the possibility of acquiring offshore investment. Taking his money to the Channel Isles – Guernsey, that was the place to be. And ....what an ideal reason to go away. In true James Bond style he began to plan again. The business was running reasonably well and as far as he was concerned he had a colleague in the office at the time, who he thought he could trust to run the business. John, he felt was quite capable of running the business, especially from the monetary point of view. And he, well he was putting the icing on the cake as it were.

Freddie suggested to Helen that she think of an excuse to tell her family and of course her boyfriend, as to the reason why she was going away for several days, on a business trip to Guernsey. Since she was his Personal Assistant, this should not prove to be too difficult. She was his right arm, everyone knew that. Everyone knew how he had come to depend on her. He needed her there with him, to provide important information, information to which, frequently as his assistant she had every access. Rather than his right arm in fact, she was more like the right side of his brain. All the details were arranged; everything should run smoothly while he was away, both at work and at home.

Thursday couldn't come quick enough, not for him anyway. He waited anxiously, almost impatiently for her, when he arrived to pick her up. She was taking an absolute age. Had she changed her mind?

He wondered. Would he be able to bear it if she changed her mind now? What was he going to do if she didn't turn up? Panic began to set in.

But there was no way, I mean no way, she was going to let him down. Here she came, suitcase in hand looking as radiant, as beautiful as ever. She knew how to turn a man's head. She knew how to choose just the right clothes to accentuate her firm and formly shape. She knew just the right colours to enhance her own colouring. For one so young, she was experienced and mature in many ways. He felt his heart miss a beat as she got into the car. It missed a beat from the thought of what might not have been.

They raced to Birmingham airport, as if there was no time to lose. Only the best of course – first class seats on the plane. Helen was particularly excited. He hadn't realised at first just how important this trip was for her, until he found out it was actually her first time on a plane. He couldn't believe his luck. There was Helen, the light of his life, the woman he loved, sitting by his side. He felt a kind of warmth within himself, a sort of glow, a feeling. It was difficult to describe. Was the heat radiating from her? Was the warmth coming from himself? Or once again, perhaps it was the electric currents which were radiating energy from each body in waves, sending signals of their nearness, of their need for each other. One thing was certain, if they weren't careful, they'd be sending smoke signals, for all to see.

A warm, balmy breeze greeted them at the airport in Guernsey. The hotel, the St Pierre Park was magnificent and that was just from the outside. Five star of course – it had everything. Five star in every shape and form. They were greeted warmly at reception. Their bags were carried and they were guided quietly to their room.

The lift itself set the scene, for what was to be a memorable time. So shiny, you could view your reflection in its walls, to some this might not be acceptable, however, and it gave Freddie ample views of Helen from all sides. He simply couldn't take his eyes off her. Then to the corridors, they were just as plush, with thick pile carpet and when we talk of thick, well it was so thick, it would have needed a chain saw to cut it in two. But this was just a taste of what was to come.

Arriving at their room, they realised exactly what they were there for. A most ostentatious room, sumptuously and luxuriously furnished. A glamorous room, with an en suite bathroom which was just as large and which suffered the vanity of a massive, oceanic sized bath and everything came with gold plated fittings. The room itself, enormous as it was, had the most beautiful bounteous sized central bed. Huge in all its proportions. In fact you would have needed a pair of step ladders just to climb into it. He could just imagine a riotous night of sex in this bed, one turn too many and you might find yourself in a hospital bed.

Their journey had been, in his words, "Just simply knackering". He couldn't in fact believe that he had travelled all this way to be with Helen and now he was absolutely shattered. It passed through his mind. What if he couldn't perform as well as he had before? What if he fell asleep? Would she laugh? Would she find him ridiculous? Perhaps believe him to be old and past it! Still, it's amazing isn't it, just where you can get your strength from when it's most needed? He really needn't have worried. Not with his Helen there beside him.

They decided; not unsurprisingly to retire to bed quite early. Helen made her way to the dressing room. Freddie waited and he waited. But by God was the wait well worth it! When Helen emerged from the dressing room, she was wearing the most incredible outfit. The most luminous, clinging negligee he had ever set eyes upon. It accentuated her whole figure – or it might be more appropriate to say it displayed her whole figure.

Surely her family were by now quite suspicious. Surely her family must have gathered by now what was going on between them. They could not have helped but notice the clothes she brought with her on this trip. This negligee they could not have missed.

That night was one you might say, never to be repeated again. Every single time however, he made love to Helen; it seemed to be an experience in itself. On reflection now in fact, not once in the ten years he knew her intimately, was sex to become boring and repetitive. It was a trip to heaven by an entirely different route. As far as he was concerned, at that time, she was without doubt an angel sent from heaven for him, even though it was for a short time.

He thought back now to this time with wonder. Sometimes with fondness and warmth, at other times with sadness and anger.

8

The Magic Isles

Guernsey was to be just one of the magic places Freddie would spend time with his princess, his nymphet and she would conjure up more than just a little magic into his life, with offerings from her own sweet magic isles.

Having slept but briefly on their first night of arrival in Guernsey, they decided to take a light, fast breakfast in order to take in more of the delights of the hotel and of the island. There was said to be a beautiful swimming pool based within the hotel complex, this they had to try out, just for relaxation's sake on their first day. It might help them unwind from their tiring journey. Down they went to try out the swimming pool. Of course, it had everything, including a small Jacuzzi, which was hidden away in a corner of the swimming pool surrounded by Romanesque pillars. Of course, it was the Jacuzzi which was most tempting; they just had to try it out.

Helen was dressed in an exceptional figure hugging bikini. In fact it was a bikini which said "Please hug me!" – An invitation that wasn't needed. But hell she did have quite a figure! A figure of ample, though easy proportions – it was a curvy 38-24-38 figure, with legs that went straight up to her ears. He couldn't remove his eyes from her as she stepped seductively into the Jacuzzi. The look on her face was provocative in itself. She was an utter temptress. She had a "dare you, dare me!" expression.

This beautiful creature was his, all his, he couldn't believe his luck. He looked around to see if anyone was looking. Was anyone else eyeing her up in the same way? Was anyone coveting the woman he loved? He was ready to argue with anyone who was. His mind was very definitely wandering, it was elsewhere. He was in a trance. In a world all of his own.

Once in the Jacuzzi, Helen crept closer to him, savouring the warmth, the tingling sensation provided by the bubbles. Her hands crept under the water, first to his waist, pinching him, prodding him playfully, she caught him unawares. Then her hands began wandering over him, wandering down to parts that were sensitised, to parts that other hands she hoped couldn't reach. To an area that was accentuated all at once. He came back sharply to the land of the living. In a conscious state, he whispered to her that if she continued, things would develop there, then in public. He wouldn't be able to help himself. She just smiled sweetly and then she continued. She was like that. And .... well he couldn't help himself.

He was overtaken by desire; he could contain his feelings, his urge no longer. He reached down, slowly, though urgently, tracing the edge of her bikini bottom with his fingers. Testing to see if she was just toying with him, with his emotions. Would she dare to take a chance here in public? She wasn't playing; her urge was as great as his. Taking first a precautious note of his surroundings, to see if anyone was around, because he wasn't given to exhibitionism, he slowly urged her bikini bottom down. No one would see anything he was sure, not with all these bubbles. No one was around anyway.

He slid slowly over to her, almost in a time warp.

The exhaustion from their travels drained away. The bubbles from the Jacuzzi acting almost like the bubbles from a champagne bottle, going straight to their heads, they made love there and then. It was a hurried, furtive, but exhilarating love making.

Afterwards there appeared no need for hurry. She kissed him. A sweet, innocent kiss, as if nothing had happened. But the tingling sensation remained within their bodies. A sensation not created by the bubbles, but by a glow from each other of satisfaction.

The first few days at Guernsey were meant to be for them. Not for business. Not for work. Just for them. Dinner at the hotel was not a timid affair. It was a culinary delight, a feast in itself. Everyone dressed up for the occasion and although Helen was still sponsoring her own lifestyle, her dress sense fitted in well with the surroundings. She wore a beautiful, long, flowing virginal evening dress. Freddie of course, in true James Bond style – sported a white tuxedo dressed with cufflinks. The Victor Hugo suite was no ordinary suite; only A la Carte menus were served. A romantic first class meal consisting of caviar, steak Diane and for Helen - well she chose oysters. He had to admit at this point in time, there was no way she needed those oysters. Champagne and a lovers Torte was to be the compromise and finale for both of them. And at the very end, all was rounded off with the usual spirits, liqueurs, coffee, cheese and biscuits.

What could follow such an overwhelming meal? Except of course............ Meanwhile, back in the suite that night, back in the huge bed made only for a giant – or in this case made for giant lovers. They were not prepared to waste either their time together, or this beautiful bed. An evening, a night, a morning all of love making. They were like a couple on honeymoon, it was an incredible time. It was a time that money could not buy, it was a time that if he had not been so avaricious, so vain, he would have realised that money cannot buy you happiness. No matter how much money you have. But Freddie was living in his own little world, a world viewed through rose coloured glasses. Some might say he was living in a fool's paradise. But he didn't care. Why should he? He had plenty of money. He had the woman he loved. Why should he care?

Their time in Guernsey really was a time of magic and a time of mysticism. Apart from their magical love making, the places they visited together were also mystical, providing them with a sense of togetherness, a sense that they were in their own little world. A trip to St Peter's Port harbour in Guernsey on the weekend resulted in a short journey by hydrofoil to the ancient walled French city of St Malo.

A beautiful, Breton port town on the north coast, St Malo is surrounded by a Napoleonic fortified wall. Passing through one of the largest arches in the wall, you enter a time gone by. It is a town of cobbled streets, medieval, tall buildings which overpower the walkway and shops and restaurants galore. It contains shops of every description, from beautiful craft shops of leather, jewellery and pottery, perfume shops and delicatessen, to pizza houses and A la carte restaurants. St Malo, a town of warmth and happiness, of hustle and bustle. All these things added even more magic, more closeness to their time together.

Then, it was on to the medieval, mystical, Gothic town of St Michael's Mount or Mont St Michel, if you are French. A town dating back to a time almost forgotten. To a time before the English and French wars, before Joan of Arc, before the great French "Sun" King Louis.

When the sea is out, which is most of the time these days, Mont St Michel can be approached from the end of a vast causeway. Visitors in their thousands can be seen arriving and then leaving their cars on the car parks on the edge of the mainland. Walking up the miles of causeway, you feel a sense of something, a sense of the unknown, a sense of wonder. As you observe the huge circular mound arising from the sand bank, growing before your very eyes and circled by several smaller pawns, you can't help but be amazed by the greatness of it all. Walking up the causeway you get a sense of awe, a sense of majesty, a feeling that a medieval pilgrim or beggar might have felt, as he staggered along towards the fortification. You can't help but be aware of the same mysticism which permeates the air.

The town protected by a huge circular wall, can be accessed only through a gate in that wall. The circular formation of the town is capped, with an over impressive cathedral church and monastery at the top of its pinnacle. Once through the gate, the narrow, winding cobbled lanes are over protected by the close fitting, tall, dark buildings, the first floor of which frequently overhangs the street below. It was almost possible to picture the medieval routine, the domestic scenes which permeated these buildings. The small wooden stalls displaying wares to the customers, protected by the first floor balcony. The tardy animals, the bedraggled children running down the street, in competition with the domestic sewerage. Even the smell began to be positively medieval and the sounds, they were the sounds of the pilgrims who were punished and scourged through the streets. They were the sounds of the innocent victims of Christian fanaticism, dragged screaming to the heights of the church, in order to declare their unproved heresy against their wishes.

In the Good/Bad former days

Fred with Frank Carson

Fred ready for his dive

Les Dawson meets Fred

Fred pre-dive on the Calypso

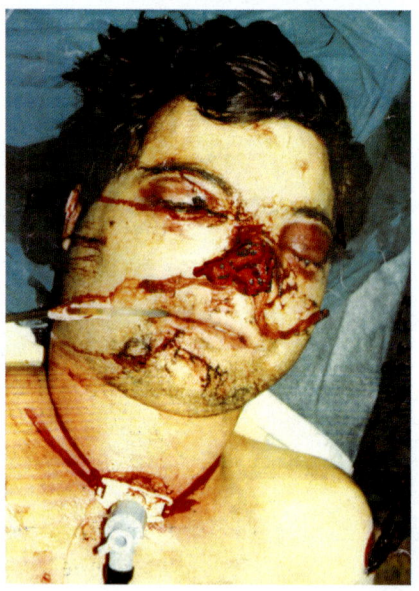

How the mighty have fallen

Most of these buildings were now souvenir shops. But one couldn't help imagining.

A tour around the timeless town, around the meticulously built monastery, down into the depths of a cold crypt where the buttressed arches were almost as large as the island itself, all of these things added magic to the whole trip. But the greatest magic was provided with the climb to the peak and looking out over the bay to the other much smaller, circular islands, whilst still under the shadow, the sanctity of the church. It was in the church that Freddie decided it was time to make some rather quiet dedication. The promise he made was to Helen. He promised that they would, if things continued to work out as they were, if things progressed as they should – they would hold their wedding in the church on St Michaels Mount. Nothing was too grand for his Helen. He would spend any amount of money that was needed to keep her happy. Their trip back was quiet, subdued, but harmonious. They vowed they would return to France as soon as possible.

It wasn't to be too long in fact. The continued expansion of Poseidon, particularly abroad, meant of course that Freddie and Helen could continue their very valuable time together. He would set up the deals; she would go along with him as his secretary, charming his associates. It didn't matter that she couldn't speak the language of the particular country that they were visiting, she was there as his secretary, his right arm.

His return from Guernsey meant of course, that he had to make up for lost time, buying metal that was either scrap or that had been on the shelf so long that no one would recognise it anyway. Not that they had any use for this scrap, most companies did not look that far ahead. The scrap usually took up very much needed space, so they were glad to get rid of it. As a result Freddie acquired some very good metal, which did not have certificates of originality, but which he could supply at a better price than other stockholders. He felt a little like "Burglar Bill".

It was this secondary metal which gave him the opportunity to travel abroad again. To France once more, but this time to the capital and obviously with his secretary. The weather as usual was wonderful. The sun always seemed to shine when he was around Helen. Although, he had to confess, he didn't spend much time worrying about the weather, in fact he didn't really notice it, except to say that it brought Helen out in the skimpiest of dresses.

Arriving in Paris, they booked into the Hotel Emeraude. A fair hotel, not as lavish as the previous one on Guernsey had been, but ....well, what did they care. As usual their time was spent, not just in business, but in a variety of aspects, including sightseeing. Helen in particular could not get enough of the sights; she was in awe of them all.

A visit to Le Sacre Coeur, a leisurely walk hand in hand, along the tree lined avenues of the Seine, mesmerised by the artists painting the local views. And here he had brought his own beautiful view, to a beautiful city. They couldn't resist the tremendous climb to the top of La Tour Eiffel; the picture from there was breath taking, one to be remembered forever and one which stretched out way beyond their imagination.

Down again, with their feet on the ground and they were off to the Champs Elysee, eyeing the current Paris fashions for the ladies. Fortunately, Freddie observed that as it was Sunday they were all shut. The prices were phenomenal, definitely not High Street Birmingham prices. He might be much better off than he ever had been, but he was still not a millionaire. Well, not yet anyway. He must be careful. At one of the cafes in the Boulevard, they sat and rested, not just their legs, but also their eyes upon each other.

Then, it was on to the place that he couldn't possibly miss – Le Louvre. Of course, he had to take Helen, his princess, his masterpiece, to Le Louvre, since that was where the masterpiece the Mona Lisa was hung. He wanted them to meet, so that he could compare their beauty. He wondered which one would be more priceless. For him there was no contest.

They returned to their hotel to freshen, amongst other more obvious things of course. Then, while she freshened again, he went off to book a table at THE famous Maxim's, where everyone who was anyone was said to frequent. Arriving by taxi, Maxim's from the outside at any rate, was not an impressive place he decided. And, on the inside, well it resembled little more than an underground railway station, with tables dotted about the room. He was not impressed in the least, since it proved to be neither a practical meal, nor an inexpensive one by any stretch of the imagination. In fact, the cheapest bottle of wine was to cost him £17. By today's standards that is excessive, in 1983, well! He was staggered to find that Maxim's had a limit; their dearest bottle of wine was in fact £400, so he felt actually that he shouldn't complain at his portly £17.

The meal was fairly sumptuous, though not distinctive, with Helen being daring and attempting the escargot; he was not so brave, sticking merely to his favourite meal of steak – no matter how it was cooked. At the end of the night the staggering bill of £180 was presented to him. An enormous sum he felt, for a meal which was not particularly distinctive, in a place though famous, that had no famous faces to show on that night. Still, at least they could say that they had been to the great Maxim's and besides, as long as Helen was happy, so was he. Nothing was too good for his princess.

They returned partly on foot to their hotel, so as not to miss the magic city lights. They felt ecstatic, what with the wine and the warmth of the night and also with each other's closeness. The lights in Paris at that time of night were incredible and added even more to their joy and sensation. Back at the hotel, they climbed sleepily into bed, though not to sleep. Of course not. They sat and talked? Of course they didn't! They made love. They made love on the bed. They made love out of the bed. They made love on the floor. Then Helen walked slowly to the bathroom and filled the bath. For relaxation she said, but they made love in the bath too. Slowly, intimately and with liquid warmth, they made love. Drowning in each other's closeness, in each other's arms, they made love. He was madly, deeply in love. What more could he want? His whole life revolved around Helen.

Business was concluded successfully, but nevertheless quickly, the following day they were to return home. However, due to extremely poor weather conditions, their flight was diverted to Heathrow instead of Birmingham. He had to return to his business, he had important business meetings to attend. Okay, so the airport authorities had laid on a coach to take them to their destination, but that was not good enough, not for Freddie. He complained. He complained so loud that the airport authorities hired him a car. Well, after all it was their problem, not his; he had booked in good faith.

They returned to the office at the ungodly hour of

10 o clock, extremely late for Freddie. John Hammond sarcastically pointed out the time and asked what the hell he, Freddie thought he was doing, particularly taking Helen away from her duties. This was the beginning of the end. How dare, this lazy slob criticise his bad timing. How dare he! Freddie exploded. What the hell gave this lazy bastard the right to criticise him? Any other person, he pointed out would have kicked him out of the business long ago. He was lucky he still had a job, let alone a partner and one who was understanding until now. He threatened him and challenged his unproductivity.

In fact, Freddie did not take him seriously at all, since by this time he had already begun to realise what was going on, that John was actually taking more from the business than he should have been. He was definitely taking much more than Freddie, but Freddie could not be sure just how much. What Freddie was sure of, was that John was still unaware of the affair between Helen and himself. He probably wasn't even clever enough to work that one out. But for the time being that's the way Freddie wanted it to stay. What to do with John was a problem though, apart from being a corporate liability, he was also an obstacle to Freddie's future well being and happiness. It was at this point that the relationship between Helen and Freddie was put on hold, purely to await any possible developments to the scene, which had taken place, but perhaps also to test their feelings for one another.

9

Samson and Delilah

Basically, the interposition of John into his personal life resulted in the downward mobility of the business relationship – if there ever had been a relationship in the first place. Something crucial must be done and soon, if the business itself was not to suffer. But more than that, much more than that, some conclusion must be arrived at, with regard to the question of the relationship between Helen and him. The interruption had only served to pinpoint severely, certain dangers which existed in the current situation.

Helen's relationship and engagement to her fiancé, was still ongoing. In fact, the wedding day was creeping incredibly close – June 17th in fact. As far as Freddie was concerned, this was one terrible blow. His mind was in turmoil. He was torn, unsure which way to turn. If he stayed with Helen, he knew he risked losing his business, his great Poseidon, his empire which he'd worked so hard to build. And then, well of course, there were his children and his wife, his house, his cars, his………. Which way to turn, that was the problem. Although, it didn't detract from the knife which turned slowly, sharply inside his body, inside his heart, each time he thought about Helen getting married. When all was said and done, the real problem was that he really hadn't got the guts, the balls to make the decision to leave. But to leave what, that was the problem!

The wedding was still going ahead. There was nothing nothing at all that he could do to stop this memorable event and he meant memorable in more ways than one. In fact if anything, he felt it would have been quite wrong of him to do so, particularly, since at this stage he had nothing substantial on the table to offer Helen in return. He wasn't all self. Not all the time anyway. He remembered quite well now, there was a record in the charts at this particular time that was very popular, even more so for Freddie. He remembered it very well indeed, as did many lovers. It was "I just called to say I love you" and one of the many lines in the song was "No wedding day in June". How ironic. How very coincidental. How could he ever forget? That was the month she, his Mona Lisa, his priceless painting, was due to marry.

Of course, the secret liaisons could not go unmissed by Gabrielle forever; she was bound to notice eventually. Bound to spot the difference in his character, in his attitude. It couldn't always be put down to hard work. Although, she was still unsure just how serious the affair was, if that's exactly what it was. He knew he was hurting her, but what could he do? He hadn't intended this to happen. It had just happened. It had slowly crept upon him, without him realising. This was perhaps another good reason for sitting back for a while, to take a check upon this new relationship within his life. If he decided to leave, it would be a big step. A big decision.

He arranged to go away with Gabrielle and the boys to Spain. That's what he needed, a little time away with his family. Get to know them again. Perhaps, things could get back to normal. He'd been under extreme pressure, working so very hard, keen to build up the business. Then there was Hammond, his partner giving him a hard time and being more than just a little shady in his private and business dealings. Yes! That was it; they needed time together to build bridges.

Of course, it wasn't just his decision that was needed. Oh no! He made it clear to Helen at the time, that if she was going to marry Phil, then it had to be her decision. Not a jot of interference from himself, in any form whatsoever. It was her decision that mattered. If she chose, their relationship would end. Obviously, he could offer her nothing at this point in time; it was only fair he let her go. It might kill him. It might kill her. But there were others to consider. By this time of course Helen's family were fully aware of their er-r somewhat less than businesslike relationship. Well, I mean to say, how could they not know, when she insisted on taking flimsy negligees to business meetings. It didn't take a lot of savvy for them to cotton on! Of course, she would no doubt be railroaded into marrying Phil. It was the right thing to do, since they knew also that he, Freddie, could or would offer her nothing in return.

And what of Phil? Well, if Phil was aware of the affair, then he must have loved her enough to forgive and forget. Well, it was always a possibility.

Yes, he must get away. He would go on holiday with his family and he really would try to pull his life back together. And she? Well, Helen would get married. She would go on her honeymoon and try to put her life back into some sort of order. Along with his family, on their trip to sunny Spain, came some long standing friends of his and Gabrielle's. They all knew the score. He felt that their presence at this particular time would be very important in helping him to get everything in perspective again. After all, his family were an alternative to Helen, or vice versa and therefore one would always be a reminder of the other. So far as he was concerned, it was very much the more the merrier on this particular trip.

The holiday really couldn't have been better, in some respects. A luxurious villa shared by one and all, near to Marbella. Nightlife, day life – all for the taking. Pleasure trips, boat trips – they couldn't want for more. They took the trip of a lifetime to a beautiful Castellan village called Rhonda. The approach to Rhonda itself was magnificent. Driving down from Marbella, through the beautiful town of San Pedro, you follow the road to Rhonda, a spiralling drive around mountain roads, round hairpin bends, until you arrive on the top of a very large precipice. This was Rhonda, in all its splendour. A town perched as a crow's nest, high on the mountain top. Where you can look down on to some of the most incredible views.

Everything below in miniature. He remembered thinking at the time, for a person who was hell bent on suicide, this was their paradise. This is where he found himself on the Saturday that Helen was due to get married. All the time thinking about her, about some of the beautiful trips they had made together.

He found himself in a sort of trance, a coma like state. Just wandering around, everyone wondering why, on such a beautiful day, in such a beautiful place, he should be in an awful shit of a mood. Well, they were aware of the reason, but they were beginning to be a little impatient as to why he couldn't snap himself out of it. After all, he had chosen to go on this holiday, now he was spoiling it for everyone. But he, well he felt, as if he had lost everything.

He was getting desperate, desperate for a telephone, desperate because the time of her wedding was drawing closer. He became more morose, more depressed with every second that passed. Phil, one of the friends who had gone on holiday with Freddie and his family, came to ask what the matter was. But Phil knew the score. He couldn't even get away from a name that was connected to Helen; even Freddie's best friend had the same name as her fiancé.

Twelve thirty came, then twelve thirty five, then finally the church bell rang out the dreaded time thirteen hundred hours No, not one o clock, it had to be that dreaded figure thirteen, unlucky for some, but definitely unlucky for him, because this was his deadline to find a telephone. He was 3,000 miles away and he could do nothing about it. He could do nothing at all. He could just see her now, all dressed in her virginal white wedding dress, arriving at the church in Brierley Hill in the West Midlands. And what could he do? He could do nothing. Nothing to stop his fairytale princess from marrying the ugly toad. The great Freddie Jones, could not get to a telephone, he couldn't even buy one, he couldn't contact her and say "Freeze, hold it there, I can't live without you". He had lost her, lost her forever.

Sometime later, she mentioned to him, that had he rung her, rung her for any reason whatever, whether it was to tell her that she'd made the right decision, or the wrong decision, he would have stopped her dead in her tracks. All she needed was to hear the sound of his voice. But most of all she wanted to hear, funnily enough, exactly what he had wanted to say – that he wanted her, wanted her above all else. Who knows what would have happened had she not gone ahead with the wedding. But Freddie carried on with his holiday, knowing she was now a married woman, not knowing what she was thinking. He carried on with his holiday, even though it wasn't the best holiday he had ever experienced, or the worst for that matter, but it was certainly the most unusual holiday he had ever had.

To think that at that time, he had the money just to jump back on the plane, to go home, to ask Helen to be his. But he didn't, he thought about it. But he didn't. What had held him back? His mind had been in an utter turmoil, he didn't know what to do, he knew what he wanted to do, but not what to do. He wanted Helen. He wanted someone who had never meant anything to him as much as she had. To him, she was the goddess of love, of affection, of emotion. He felt it hard to believe that anyone had ever experienced anything quite as he had. It had changed his whole life, his destiny.

He arrived back off holiday, sun-tanned, bronzed. Helen also returned back from her honeymoon, nicely tanned, pleasant and just as beautiful as ever. But with a certain hesitation about her. He probably appeared the same to her, but he didn't feel it himself. In fact, his feelings if they were anything to go by were in the process of an almighty argument with his senses, with what he knew was right.

The first day back in the office was the worst. At first they walked around each other, almost as if the other were an apparition, to be seen, but to be avoided. They tried desperately to avoid eye contact, but their desperation was in vain. Finally, their eyes crept around to meet, drawn by curiosity, they acknowledged each other.

Communication until now had been fairly non-existent, with barely a "Good Morning Mr Jones" and a "Good Morning Mrs Wright" in return. The Mr and Mrs being deliberately accentuated to emphasise the new status. But it wasn't to be as simple as that. Oh no. Their eyes gave away much more than anything else. They both knew that they should, that they had to live their own lives. Helen with her new married life, Freddie with his new determination to succeed in resurrecting his marriage, his life with Gabrielle and the boys, to be revamped and upstaged. But their feelings, their eyes told a very different story. They knew there and then that they could not let this thing, this old passion just die.

They tried hard at first to ignore the situation, pretending nothing had happened between them. They went back to business, back to what they were good at, for Freddie that was buying and selling, using his gift of the gab. For Helen that meant typing, secretarial duties and communicating with people at the office – the things at which she was good. They conducted themselves impeccably, much to the sheer amazement of everyone around, for of course, by this time, everyone who was anyone knew what had been going on. They went from day to day in a sort of mesmerised trance. Well, that is to say they lasted the remarkable sum of exactly two days. By the third day, Freddie resolved to silence the quiet! He could wait no longer. He decided the situation was totally ridiculous. They were acting like complete strangers and no one who had been as close as they had, could possibly operate efficiently under these circumstances. Freddie just had to say something, he was being torn apart and business was suffering.

Funnily enough, it hadn't been as tough as he had at first thought it might be. Helen made it easier, by agreeing that she too was in turmoil, knowing full well what she should do, but incapable of carrying out tasks. She didn't know which way to turn.

They decided to go out and talk about their dire situation over lunch. Freddie took Helen to what is now known as the Renaissance, at Coven in Wolverhampton. They stopped off at a little pub on the way, to discuss the various things that stood in their way of tackling everyday life. The fact that they were both now married; that there were other people who could get hurt. Everything that had been discussed by the two, prior to Helen's marriage was reiterated, re-emphasised, as if they were trying to convince themselves.

They sat in a discreet corner of the room, in order to avoid attention and in order to discuss their problems. Their eyes met over the round table and the discreteness of the corner gave way to a rashness that only Sir Lancelot and Queen Guinevere could have known. First their eyes met and then the magnetism played upon their hands, drawn together, eyes met again and then lips. At first a gentle, tender, sweet kiss; then with the sparks igniting the electric situation, a more devastating, soul searching, passionate, suffering kiss. A kiss that seemed to have waited an eternity, they had been apart for too long. There appeared no power on this earth that could have stopped them from coming together. Not now, not ever.

So lost in love for each other, they could not remember getting back into the car. But to this day they could remember the magic of the moment which had edged the car into a golden hayfield, drawn it to a stop and motioned to them to get out. Slowly, they got out of the car. They lay down in this beautiful hayfield, a hayfield which was made even more beautiful because of its consequence of that day and they made love. Not just a gentle, soul searching love, but a mad, passionate, imploring, "miss you" love. It was an urgent, yet delicate and intimate love. They could do nothing else. They had no power to stop the situation. They knew then that they were committed to each other. To think that, essentially just ten days after Helen was married, the two of them would be making love in a hayfield on the outskirts of Wolverhampton. This was not opportunism. It was not lust. It was about two people, who very passionately loved each other and who were keen to show each other just how much.

Things got back to normal. Well, normal by the standards they had been before Helen got married. Freddie, well he arranged a trip. Right, you've guessed, what else but a trip abroad. Of course, it was meant to be a business trip, a trip to Italy and Helen, well she didn't go along just for the ride, she went along as his secretary of course They flew to Sorrento. A fairytale place, very similar in natural structure to the high cliffs and coasts of Cornwall, except that it was very much larger.

The people in Sorrento, like the weather, were warm and friendly. They booked into the Hotel Esmerelde. It would prove to be a holiday, if not like all the others, then more mind blowing, more exciting than the others. At the Hotel Esmerelde, they met what can only be described as the spitting image of the members of the A-team, that corny old serial from 1980's television. Murdoch acted as one of the waiters, Face served behind the bar and completing the team was someone called Alan Smith who helped to staff the hotel. He just happened to be the spitting image of B.A. Barracus. It was one hell of a holiday, almost like a honeymoon again without the marriage.

Italians love lovers. Helen and Freddie were no exception to the rule. The Italians loved them. Helen and Freddie spent the hottest part of the day locked away in their bedroom apartment. They could have pretended that they were enjoying their siesta, but they had no intention of hiding what they were really enjoying. They were enjoying being in love. They were enjoying making love. The whole of the time there was one long fabulous period of lovemaking. What had been left out of the Karma Sutra was invented and included by these two love birds.

Helen's complete and utter desire was to go on a journey

through Rome. After all, what was Italy without a visit to the most important sites and cities – Sorrento, Rome, Pompeii, Venice – she wanted to see them all. They took a bus to Rome to see the Catholic Capital – the Vatican City. They found themselves in awe of the most grandiose, though rather cold Italian Renaissance masterpiece – St Peter's Basilica. Its vastness covering some four acres of land, three times the size of the Notre Dame of Paris. The interior creating an impression of majestic serenity, with its gilded and ornate decoration and the marvellous, larger than life paintings by Michelangelo.

It was an ideal time of the year to go, the Italians were on holiday, there were no massive queues. They saw the splendid windows of St Paul's, the architecture was phenomenal, the paintings on the ceilings utterly incredible.

Of course, they couldn't leave Rome without a visit to the famous Trevi Fountain. The fountain of lovers, where a toss of the coin into the water ensures that wishes come true, mind you only the wishes of lovers. So, of course, Freddie and Helen couldn't resist a toss, or two – just to ensure success. There was so much more to see, the beautiful central park, just made for lovers, where they could visit the Roman Temple, the beautiful Villa Bourgoizy, situated on an island in the centre of a huge lake. They could hire a boat and row to the temple; they could pledge their undying love for one another. They could visit the church, where all prayers are answered, purely by praying as you pass upon each step.

Rome the city where the past comes to life. With more monuments and busts than possibly any other city. In fact, probably more busts than you would find in a feature length film of Baywatch. Rome the city of Christianity, but where the contrasts between the rich and the poor are so vast. The beautiful churches adorned with mosaic, marble and masterpieces from times no longer remembered. The city with its narrow streets and tall dark concrete buildings, where beggars sit astride the pavements. Rome the city of contrasts, where anybody, who is anybody has visited – Julius Caesar, Caligula, Nero, John Keats, Byron, Shelley. A city famous for its solid mixture of poetry and politics. But for Freddie and Helen, there wasn't time to see everything.

They visited cameo factories. They went to Pompeii to see the ruins of a town left devastated by the eruption of Mount Vesuvius - a shattering and mind blowing experience. On the way back, they stopped at a place that was apparently famous in Sorrento for making the world's largest pizzas. There was so much to see, toy factories, inlaid marquetry tables and beautiful furniture. The ice creams spoke for themselves.

Back at the hotel, they were treated like royalty. Even though they weren't married. To the Italians this made no difference. They, Freddie and Helen, Helen and Freddie, were obviously very much in love and that was all that mattered to these romantic Italians. No holds were barred. They were provided with everything – at a cost of course.

During their stay, they discussed quite seriously, their future and made some very definite plans. In fact, if anything, Helen's plans were probably much more definite than Freddie's. After all she had waited for so long for Freddie, for him to leave his wife and children, for him to move in with her. She wanted him with her all the time; she wanted him home with her in the evenings. Freddie on the other hand had procrastinated – because of Gabrielle, because of the children, perhaps because of Poseidon? Who knew? They discussed what they were going to do. How they were going to do it. What sort of timetable they would set themselves. They tried to steal themselves to discuss what they really wanted at that time. That was to be together.

He recalled now, other times they had spent together. Like the time they spent the night together at the Chateau Impney in Droitwich. Calling in on spec without a reservation, because they became desperate to be together, to make love. Because the attraction became too great for them to deny. A rash decision which turned out quite well. As a result they had been offered the only suite available, the bridal suite!

They were always lucky with their choice of hotels. In this case, just as in the others, the room was fantastic, with a four poster bed the size of an oil platform in the North Sea. It had been an ideal setting, there in the middle of the Worcestershire countryside. In fact, it would be a time to remember, since they were to be caught unawares. A time when they would have to hide their embarrassment. But a time they would also laugh about later.

On this occasion, they had undressed and then lay on the bed, savouring at first the quiet that surrounded them. Then they savoured the sound of each other's slow laboured breathing. Freddie rolled over; he began by caressing and savouring her long smooth neck. The sensation welling up within them both, each tingling in anticipation of what was to come. However, they weren't prepared for exactly what was to come. To their surprise, the door swept wide open. Both of them froze, lay exactly where they were. Sheer shock struck home.

They were stark naked on the bed and who should walk in but the maid. Towels in hand, she walked straight in, deposited the towels and walked straight back out again. She certainly had a tremendous amount of savoir faire, she didn't seem in the least perturbed by what she had seen and she just glanced and walked away. She was either very well trained, or she was used to seeing this sort of thing most days. However, Freddie and Helen must also have had a certain amount of savoir faire. Nothing was going to stop them in mid flow, not once they had started and certainly not once the maid had left the room. They continued where they had left off.

He continued to reminisce. On another occasion, he remembered that they had gone back to Guernsey for a short break, staying at the Green Oaks hotel. They knew the owner of the hotel quite well, or at least they knew him quite well after their first visit. On the first night they came down to dinner, the owner who was also acting as head waiter that night, made a bee line for their table. He asked very quietly, if they knew of any good plasterers there in Guernsey. Freddie motioned that he didn't quite understand did he have a problem there at the hotel.

"No, no, it's nothing like that." The owner proclaimed. "It's just that this afternoon, when the two of you had gone to your room, we thought the ceiling was about to fall in over the top of the restaurant."

He motioned to roughly the area of their room. Freddie and Helen realised that he was referring to their little siesta together that afternoon and attempted to hide their embarrassment with apologies.

Later on that evening, they were presented with a large bottle of wine on the house. This was the manager's way of apologising for his little joke and for interrupting the life they were obviously enjoying. The next day, as they mounted the stairs, they called to the owner and pointed out that there was no need to call for the plasterers, since they were only changing their gear to take a tour around the island.

10
Joie de Vivre

Helen was nothing but the joy of life itself. Freddie, at this point in time, could not imagine life without Helen. Not for one minute. They went everywhere together.

They performed tasks together they never thought were possible. Those times were certainly memorable. The places they went, the things they did together, the people they met – each one important in creating a memory for one reason or another.

On the island of Guernsey, they had hired a car. They had taken a journey around the island. They enjoyed the usual things most people do on holiday – sun, sand, sea and s-s-s........ and "skiing" was what he had in mind! But I suppose it would be quite practical to go along with your original thoughts, since life would not be the same for Helen and Freddie without sex.

The journey around the island took him back to a time when he was at school. He was about fourteen or maybe fifteen years of age when he first met Alwin Bins, or at least I should say Alwin Bins the first, Alwin Bins the second was the nephew of the first and in fact attended the same school as Freddie at the time, that being Dormston High School in Sedgley. They became fairly good friends. In fact, close friends would be a more appropriate word, since they spent a considerable amount of time together.

Alwin Bins the first was a travelling gent, a guide, an

intelligent man of mature years, whose resemblance to the ecclesiastical variety was immense. It was purely by chance, or by Alwin Bins the second that he met this remarkable gent back in Sedgley, in his early years. It was no surprise, therefore, given his demeanour that this quaint gent became the vicar of Torteval in Guernsey. Freddie went purposely to seek this man out and to say it was the most wonderful reunion was purely an understatement. Alwin Bins the first was the most pleasant, charitable, sensible, remarkable man you could wish to meet, even though a little eccentric.

In the vicarage there in Torteval, he had a tiny vineyard in his conservatory, where he grew the most incredible grapes. Freddie told him that he had deliberately attempted to seek him out and Alwin made him feel exceptionally welcome. Freddie also informed him that he was on business there in Guernsey. Well, what else could he say "My dear man, I'm here on a dirty weekend with my secretary" – no, that wouldn't do, especially to someone of the "frock". Alwin invited them both over to dinner that night and probably much to the chagrin of Helen; she was introduced to Alwin as his assistant. They reminisced over the places they had visited in those early days, along with his nephew. It was indeed a most ideal end to a memorable weekend.

Freddie had gone to conduct business in Guernsey and that is exactly what he did. On his return to work, he imparted the arranged information to his partner, Hammond. Freddie had also travelled to Guernsey in order to carry out business for himself, to set up an offshore bank account. He was very careful however, not to let Hammond in on everything he did. By this time Freddie was already aware of his partner's less than correct accounting with the company funds. However, he hadn't approached him as yet, since he felt he hadn't enough evidence. But Freddie felt it was necessary to secure his own future and to set up, quite legitimately of course, business or funds of his own. Hammond was quite happy; he was getting more than his fair share. So what the heck. At the time Freddie was ecstatic, as long as he was making money, keeping Helen happy, then everything was fine and he was happy too.

As Freddie's assistant, Helen could of course acquire a car through company funds. Although the first of many cars Freddie was to buy her was out of his own pocket, after he managed a good scrap deal. It was a crazy, zany little mini which he managed to purchase fairly cheap. It was important to him at the time – to show just how much he cared for Helen – and for him, well this sealed it.

At the time when she was learning to drive, Freddie had a Ford Capri 2.8 injection, "Speed on wheels" as he called it at that time. In fact, this title suited Helen also; he liked to call her his speed on wheels. Not just because she drove dangerously and in the fast lane, but also because whenever she was near, he felt really high.

One day, when he was teaching her to drive in the Capri, she made the decision to overtake a bus that was in front. Freddie of course, sitting in the passenger seat couldn't see an awful lot and relied solely on Helen's judgement. However, when Freddie looked up, there driving towards them in the opposite direction was another bus. Freddie the fearless was no longer. It certainly didn't inspire the greatest amount of confidence in him. However, he had to admit that Helen was the greatest ride – sorry, drive around. She was fast, quick and always ready to go flat out.

Helen had mentioned to Freddie that she liked a

particular engagement ring in Samuels's jewellers in Wolverhampton. It was a second hand ring and even then it cost around £350. Ever the romantic, Freddie went in and bought the engagement ring, had it sized to her finger and then placed it carefully in the sugar bowl, under the sugar. Enticing her to have a coffee, he pulled her cup closer, reached in the sugar bowl with a spoon and there was the ring. Helen recognised the ring straightaway, though frankly it glistened so brightly in contrast to the grains of sugar, she couldn't have missed it. Amid shrieks of joy, she picked it out, looked at him with a riveting look which said it all, he placed it on her finger and then the enticing was all hers. This was err-r-r the sort of bigamist engagement of 1984.

Then there was the time they visited Vye beach, in Crete, where all the Bounty adverts are made. Vye beach is beautiful, a paradise, beyond belief or description. A pure white sandy beach, fringed with coconut palms, although it is one of the Greek islands, it is literally a tropical island. Clear blue sea, reflecting the colour of the sky, it is a gateway to heaven. Two beautiful, glorious weeks were spent on this island, during which time they visited an array of places, including the famous Temple of Knossos, with its famous legend of the great and fearless Minotaur.

Much of their time of course was spent on the beach, or in a little local taverna by the side of the beach. They frequently went skiing, well Freddie went skiing. Helen made a couple of attempts, at which she was very good. She had the ability to pick up a sport quite quickly. However, Helen decided she preferred to stick to the inflatable rings that were towed along – that was easier.

In the evenings, they visited the hillside taverns, high in the mountains, where the air was still stiflingly warm, but a cool breeze arose, just enough to cool the situation. The scenery was magnificent, particularly as the sun went down, at first huge and global, like some unknown planet coming in to take a closer look, then the sun turned to shadowing the horizon. They joined the locals, drank their ouzo, shared their food and even danced a little, although this posed some problems for Helen, who once again found herself the centre of attraction for the men. The hotel they stayed in was fantastic. In the mode of most Greek buildings, it was virginal white, built right on the beach, it was heaven itself. The food was good; the ambience warm and inviting, the nightlife was exciting. The whole fortnight spent on the island was fantastic, heaven itself. The air was warm, the scenery was beautiful and every minute of every day was an hour in itself.

When they finally returned home, they were still very much on a high, still very much in love and began looking for places that they could share, somewhere they could call their own. Freddie found an advert for a cottage in Wolverley and actually paid a deposit of £500, a deposit albeit to rent for a period of six months, he did have the option to buy at the end of this period. It was an oldie world two bed roomed cottage at 5 Wolverley Gardens, a beautiful, romantic little hideaway. At that particular point in time he, Freddie could, nay would have moved in, at least this is what he told himself. However, Helen was never aware of the situation. Although Freddie was also feeling terribly insecure by the further deceit of his partner at this time, whilst he felt he should muster all the funds he could, he was a little unsure as to whether it was the right time to make a move. Or, was he just making excuses again?

A wife, a mistress, a partner, an international business

and all of it working well – reasonably well anyway. What more could he want? Before the problems began, in his business and partnership, Hammond had actually introduced to him the secret and demanding world of the Freemasons. He, Freddie, had actually been provided at his reasonably young age with the opportunity of becoming elected as a Magistrate. Oh the power! And finally, he had taken up his teenage dream of becoming a disc jockey, albeit with a local radio station. All of this time – fame and fortune – had provided opportunities he never dreamed of, of meeting people he never thought it would be possible to meet, many of whom were to become friends and acquaintances.

Freddie had met, on many occasions, Les Dawson. In fact, on one occasion Les had actually agreed for Freddie to kidnap him. Oh, very much for a good cause, all for the benefit in fact of Stour Valley Hospital Radio. From that time on, Les and Freddie became good friends. Freddie the funny man appeared to attract a cackle of comedians, for Les was not the only one to befriend him.

On one of Freddie's many visits to Spain, he came across Frank Carson. In Freddie's usual pushy, egotistical manner, whilst dining in a restaurant in Marbella, he spotted Frank and sent a note across to his table. Freddie explained that he was from a radio station in England and would like to meet with him. The deal was clinched with a gin and tonic. They started talking and became friendlier and Frank agreed to contact Freddie, at his radio station in Stourbridge when he returned to England. Freddie thought this might be the brush off, but no, Frank was as good as his word. Don Maclean was another of the rare breed of super jokers, who took the time to get to know Freddie quite well. A comedian Freddie met through his hobby as a pilot.

His life was really taking off, not just in the fast lane, but in the funny lane too. Mind you, as they say, money does talk. Like the time, or should I say times, he went to see Lionel Richie. Both Gabrielle and Helen were keen to see this star and well, he had to be fair, he couldn't take one without the other. No, I don't mean he took them together, at the same time; he wasn't that cruel, or stupid. But he had to keep them both sweet and so he took Gabrielle one night and Helen the very next night. Although he was keen to see Richie himself. It really is incredibly fortunate when you have enough money to buy your way in and that's just what he did, bought his way back stage to see Lionel Richie.

And so, life in the fast lane continued, for a little while at least. He was madly in love with Helen and possessive of her all at the same time. He was proud to show her off, he enjoyed the looks she got from other men, but at the same time he was also insanely jealous. But it didn't stop him. It was a form of masochism if you like; he enjoyed putting himself through the torture. He took her everywhere.

In fact, he would never forget one of their final holidays together. The time they took a trip to Marbella. They stayed at a villa belonging to a friend of Freddie's from the metal trade. A beautiful villa with all the mod cons and the facilities of home, including a massive swimming pool. It was an ideal place for Helen to show off her ample charms and on the balcony, basked in the rays of the sunshine, almost like a halo around her body she would sunbathe in the nude. Of course he minded, but he was just as pleased and as awe struck by her body as everyone else. He couldn't utter a sound in protest, even though he was aware that others were ogling. Still what the heck, he had her, they didn't.

One extremely hot, sunny day, they paid a visit to the Aqua Park in Marbella. Helen wearing a bikini bottom and a tee shirt, they were about to approach the slide. The attendant however, refused them admittance, on the grounds that Helen's tee shirt could get caught up on something and result in a nasty accident. Helen not to be thwarted removed her top and the looks of all concerned around her, including the attendant, said it all. He was obviously gobsmacked by Helen's very curvaceous figure. For Freddie, it was a case of pride in the looks she got, a case of look what I've got, look who I'm with. If the attendant was worried before about an accident, now he should worry, since all the men were watching Helen and not watching where they should be going.

Whilst staying in Marbella, they visited Toni Dali's restaurant – the famous Italian opera singer. En Espana, Toni Dali's is the place to be seen and the place where you see the famous. He remembered the time well. The favourite record at the time was "Three times a lady", how could he forget, since they had been serenaded with this tune at their table. It was a most magical evening. A beautiful restaurant – candles on the table, marble floors and a fountain which sprang forth in the middle of the room. The Moorish, medieval, mosque – like building, was not only approached by pure white marble archways, but these archways appeared to cascade down like waterfalls, around the restaurant floor. Glistening glass partitions separated the restaurant from the pure white beach, which still emanated a shimmer from the afternoon heat.

Just picture a huge sunset, slowly sinking down toward the horizon. Creating a colourful halo of yellows, gold, oranges and reds around its pancake image. Imagine, the sweet scented jasmine trailing around the veranda, the bougainvilleas, the heat, the dusk, the intermingling smell of perfumes from those present, but only being aware of the musk scent of your partner. The blue of the Mediterranean turning green as the light dies down. An incredible, enchanting and certainly most romantic sight. It was a holiday to beat all holidays. It was like being in a time warp. Freddie felt extremely lucky to be alive. He had the best of everything. He wanted for nothing. Well, not at this point in time anyway.

However, things were not always to be plain sailing. This was 1985. A time when things were getting tight. Not just for Freddie, or Helen, or his family, or his partner, but for the country as a whole. The recession was truly on its way.

11

The Great Lexdeo

In 1983, at the ripe old age of 33, Freddie applied to become a Magistrate. You picture Magistrates as grey, bearded old men, frequently going bald, with tiny glasses perched on the end of their nose, gavel in hand. What on earth possessed Freddie, he didn't know at the time, it seemed the right thing to do. His way of attempting to change the process of a law he saw as unjust. To ensure a younger, more energetic mind would handle the system, perhaps to provide a greater justice. On the other hand, he was going up in the world; this would provide him with proof of originality, proof of firmness and solidarity.

It wasn't a difficult process, he sent a letter into the secretary for the Magistrates committee and they wrote back with an application form. They required initials of seconders, people who were prepared to vouch for his standards, proof of his background and so on. At this time, Freddie knew very well, Fergus Montgomery MP and John Blackburn MP. He asked them both whether they would be prepared to propose and second him as a Magistrate. As close friends, they were more than happy to help out. They wrote letters of proposal and of seconding and he then had to fill in another form, which checked everything from his inside leg measurement – the lot!

They checked everything from a criminal past, to

speeding offences or parking tickets, everything except for his dark liaisons of a double life. Freddie had one speeding offence which had taken place approximately nine years before. Well, they wrote back and said they were considering his application and that it would be processed in the normal course of events and that was that. He forgot all about it in fact, thinking he was being given the brush off, the old cold shoulder. This great man of confidence, he thought he wasn't good enough.

He went on holiday to his usual haunt, Marbella in Spain. However, when he returned at the end of July, beginning of August he found a letter waiting for him. The letter was from the Lord Chancellor's office, inviting him to go on courses to Keele University, to become a Magistrate. Of course he jumped at the chance. It was what he had been waiting for. It meant also, that he would have to sit in on various court hearings in the Midlands area such as Wolverhampton and Dudley, to gain experience and to act purely as an observer. Once this training had been undertaken, he would then go on the weekend seminars at Keele University.

These weekend seminars were of course, a readymade excuse for Freddie to be accompanied by "that other person". In fact, instead of staying at the campus at Keele University, where most of the other trainee Magistrates were billeted, he used to stay at the Trust House Forte Motel not far away – at his own expense of course. A full day of training and a full evening's "course" after dinner, what more could he possibly want? Perhaps this is the reason that he never really became brainwashed, as the other Magistrates were. After all, he wasn't socially mixing with them all in the evenings for further discussion and indoctrination. But this only occurred to him much later, when he was accustomed to sitting on the court cases.

He began, however, as his life had begun, by taking whatever was on offer and he meant to continue in this manner. On one occasion, when he went up to Keele, junction 16 on the M6 had been cordoned off for road works. This meant that while Freddie could come off at the correct point on the motorway to get to the Trust House Forte Motel for his bit of lunch time nooky, he couldn't actually get back on at the same point. And of course you've guessed right, he was already late for his meeting at the University. Well, he was bound to be late anyway – wasn't he? What could he do? Well, once again on another of his ego boosting trips, he explained very carefully to the workmen that he had a very urgent magisterial appointment to attend and that he was already running exceptionally late.

The workmen dressed in a variety of dusty, dirty apparel, boiler suits, dungarees, jeans which hung halfway down their large hips, displaying their moon craters, all huddled together for a brief meeting. What could they do? In fact they were exceedingly kind on this occasion, or was it really that they were being cautious, under the circumstances as he had expressed them, who would be surprised. They opened the cordon and let Freddie through, replacing the bollards as he passed. Freddie of course was now the only person weaving his way along the M6 southbound.

Freddie went through all the training, qualified as a Magistrate and was duly appointed and commissioned at Stafford Crown Court. He took the oath of allegiance, was introduced to the court clerk and duly took his place on the Seisdon bench, which he found very interesting from the point of view of all the different cases and criminal aspects that came before him. The cases ranged from petty pilfering to local villains. Imagine grilling someone in court, placing a huge fine on them and then meeting them whilst shopping or out and about in the evening.

He also sat with a Judge at the Crown Court at Wolverhampton, as part of his duties on appeal hearings and was required to attend the special courts on Saturdays, when the drunks had had a field day the night before.

Freddie's duties took him on a weird and wonderful journey through the justice system, what stories he could tell. Unfortunately silence must prevail, he had taken an oath and he could not break it

12

The Great God Caritas

Take a look in any dictionary and it will describe a Freemason as a person who is a member of a secret society based on brotherliness, charity and mutual aid. Ask Freddie Jones for his version of the Freemason and eventually he arrives at a very different answer.

The Freemasons are an organisation, basically devoted to the advancement of the individual. By inclusion in this exclusive club, you get to know as many people as you can, in as quick a time as possible, which will be of benefit to yourself, in either your business or your private life. John Hammond, Freddie's business partner, had been a member of this society for several years, had made all the right connections and had then introduced Freddie to the Masonic lodge.

Initially, Freddie had no intention of joining the Freemasons. For a start, he didn't know an awful lot about them and secondly, he felt he didn't really need to know an awful lot about them. It was a case of "He was all right Jack", or Freddie in this case. However, he was told that it would be helpful to his business and well, if that meant helping to build his beloved Poseidon still further, then so be it.

What Freddie couldn't come to terms with however, was the basic tenet and the terms under which the Masons carried out their work or tasks. The one alleged principle is that you do not go into Freemasonry for any personal gain. But if that was the case then how could you develop your business? This had Freddie baffled. Well, not really baffled, more a case of being at odds with the organisation, so that when they wished to terminate their relationship with Freddie, he definitely felt there was no real loss – not where hypocrisy was concerned.

Freddie's membership base, once he had been accepted was at Dormston Lodge in Wolverhampton. However, just as for the Magistrates, Freddie had first to be proposed and accepted as a member – he was proposed by John Hammond, his business partner at the time. The one difference being that to become a Magistrate, one had to go through formal training, to become a Freemason you had to go through the initiation process. To the Masons, it was quite probably a very similar process, or means to an end. This initiation process into the Masons was something akin to the initiation process that might be adopted by a group of schoolboys when setting up a "club".

The initiation process was quite long winded and Freddie thought presumably this was in order to ensure the person concerned, or Freddie himself in this case, was sincere in their intentions. Having been proposed and accepted into the brotherhood, he was prepared for the initiation ceremony. Dressed in a dark suit (James Bond style of course) black tie matching socks and white shirt, Freddie was led first to an ante room where he had been prepared to respond to several lines.

The initiate, on this occasion Freddie Jones, was prepared by the Tyler at the Lodge. Being blindfolded, Freddie was led by the Tyler to the door of the Freemasonry temple, there three distinct knocks were made on the door. The Junior Warden replied,

"Who have you there?"

At this point you are still Mr Smith, Mr Evans, or in his case Mr Jones, or whatever – not brother.

"A prepared candidate in a state of darkness, who has been well and worthily recommended, regularly proposed and approved in open lodge, now comes of his own free will and accord, properly prepared, humbly soliciting to be admitted to the mysteries and privileges of Freemasonry" replies the Tyler.

"How does he hope to obtain these privileges?" Asks the warden.

The Tyler prompts the candidate to answer with the following.

"By the help of God, being free and of good report."

Just then the Inner Guard joined in by stating,

"Halt while I report to the Worshipful Master."

At which point the Worshipful Master states his wish for the initiate to join the court. Freddie's mind wandered. Has anyone ever been turned away at this point? Probably not, he reflected. They had probably already been well and truly investigated before even getting this far. In which case, they must have investigated him beforehand. Well, he decided, they must have liked what they saw and what they heard.

Tylers, Junior Wardens, Worshipful Masters – if you think this is carrying things just a little too far, and then you're mistaken. In the Masons, they go still further with Senior Wardens, Secretary, Past Master, Grand Provincial Worshipful Masters and even a Grand Provincial Sword bearer. Mind you, you have to work your way through to the highest position if you are to make anything of yourself at all.

Those who have obtained the status of Provincial Masters and so forth, they are the ones who get to wear the coloured hats and the Freemasonry badges. They are the ones that delve into the very, very powerful, politically motivated, murky waters, where an enormous amount of secrecy goes unchallenged. He'd give his high teeth to gain just a little of the knowledge of what went on at their meetings.

Having answered correctly, Freddie was then led blindfolded, along what appeared to be a long passage. Being blindfolded, he thought at the time, probably made it appear longer than it actually was. He was led into the depths and solitude of the temple. Silent as the room was, he could sense the presence of others. The silence in fact heightened their breathing and the sound of their heartbeats, all of which echoed in his ears – his senses enhanced by the darkness. He was taken blindfolded, to stand at a particular spot and then told to kneel. His sense of anticipation was increased by his lack of knowledge as to what was going on, he hadn't been told what to expect. Freddie knelt cautiously down as he was directed. Sensing a cushion below, he attempted to place his knee upon it, toppling slightly as he did so. At this point his shirt was opened exposing his left breast. What was happening? What were they doing? Was it really necessary to tear out his heart?

He suspected some time later that the unusual process had been undertaken to ensure that they had made no mistake. They must ensure that a lady had not in fact, been admitted to the club, which was very exclusively male. They proceeded with the ceremony, asking questions, Freddie responding. The ceremony continued, the inner guard pressing the point of a sword against Freddie's chest.

"Do you feel anything?" He asked.

"Yes!" Freddie responded.

He definitely didn't need to learn this line. It was

at this point Freddie was led slowly, cautiously, into the lodge. What Freddie later knew to be huge oak doors, swung shut behind him. The Worshipful Master joined the quest, pursuing Freddie, questioning his age, his freedom and his will to enter the organisation. He challenged and enquired as to Freddie's reasoning for entering the Masons. He waffled on.

"Thus assured, I will thank you to kneel whilst the blessing of heaven is invoked on our proceedings."

The proceedings went on and on, almost like the advert for the washing machines! Now came Freddie's turn and he replied in harmony with the Master, who acted as a priest at a wedding.

"I, Freddie Jones, in the presence of the great architect of the universe, sincerely and solemnly promise that I will never reveal any part in the mysteries belonging to Masonry which have been made known to me.

I further solemnly promise that I will not write those secrets down or cause it to be done by others, these points I solemnly swear to observe, in the certain knowledge that on the violation of them, of having my tongue cut out and the bits scattered at sea at a low water mark."

The Worshipful Master went on to explain the use of the sacred writings, the square and the compass to those belonging to the sect of the Masons.

Blindfolded, shoeless, a noose around his neck and a sword at his bared breast – these represented the dangers that would have traditionally awaited him until his final hour. These were the penalties referred to; including having his tongue cut out should he disclose the secrets of Freemasonry. How many had gone before him. How many had in actual fact gone against the brotherhood?

First the initiation ceremony, then the passing ceremony, finally the liaising ceremony, each time further questions initiating further responses from Freddie. In the final ceremony, he was raised as a newly appointed Freemason and met everyone there involved in the brotherhood.

Part of the meeting following the ceremony involved a dinner. This meal was known as the Festive Board and as far as Freddie could discern, this was merely an excuse for becoming utterly legless. During the ceremony he was sworn to secrecy, given that special handshake that identified the Masons and the Freemasons handbook. This very secret handbook – the one especially provided for the ceremony that is – contained the rites of the ceremony. The words of course, were however missed out, making provision only for the first letter. A little silly really, since it was quite easy to make out the necessary words. Freddie felt quite honestly that it was "all a load of old cobblers". But of course he'd come this far and he felt that he had to go through with it. Reflecting now upon this period in his life, he could not work out why he had felt any sense of commitment at all.

Each lodge meeting was basically the same. Everyone concerned would be herded into the inner temple and would then be required to go through the ceremony set by the Master concerned. Everybody was required to learn their individual parts and it was impressed upon them just how important this was and how seriously it should be taken. Even more staggering was the sheer honour placed upon a visit, if the lodge was really lucky, from the Provincial Grand Master. As far as Freddie was concerned, you couldn't wish to meet a bigger load of toss pots. They were the most self-opinionated, egotistical, trainee Hitlers'; you could ever wish to meet. Now, as for the egotistical, you would have thought Freddie would have been a good match, but no they far outweighed any ability he had. Perhaps this is why he had initially felt drawn to them. But now he was no longer the King Pin!

These giant tyrants ponced around with their aprons and collarettes on, their regalia of Mastership, all of which far outweighed their actual value. Everyone else within the lodge was expected to bow and scrape to them, address them as "Your Worshipful Master" – the biggest load of cobblers out. Basically it was a great excuse for these alleged bigwigs and they were only bigwigs in Freemasonry, not in anything else, to politically and socially climb. As far as Freddie was concerned, they climbed within the Freemasons because they hadn't got the balls to climb in the real world.

Essentially, as far as he could make out there was no mystery to the club whatsoever. Anyway, he felt it was very much an organisation that could and was used to influence peoples' lives.

How the hell was Freddie going to know who was a Freemason and who was not? Quite simple really. Apart from the handshake of course, to find out if the person was on the square so to speak, it was simply a matter of saying "I was always taught to be cautious". Then if the other person was a Freemason, they would know you were being straight with them. Of course, if they weren't a Freemason, this wouldn't mean a damn thing to them, it wouldn't be of the slightest significance. If they were a Freemason however, their reply would be "Oh, you are on the square then", then they would continue by stating the number of the lodge to which they belonged.

Now, whilst the ladies were not normally admitted within the lodge setting, one of the biggest occasions was to have a ladies night. This was traditionally the night when all the ladies were invited. Wives, girlfriends and yes even mistresses for some. It was the evening when all the tables were set out in the hall and pride of place went to the Worshipful Master and his wife. It was a very glitzy sort of affair, organised traditionally to bring the "family" together, but utilised by all and sundry to see who could outdo who. You could actually see the prima donnas strutting and jockeying for the best position to gain admiring glances, to gain attention. The most outrageously expensive dresses, the bank vault jewellery all came out, with the attempt to impress or to conquer.

Even on ladies night, which was meant to be for relaxation, for fun, you would vie for a place in the limelight. You would attempt to find out who was there, what they did, how they did it and what influence and what benefit it would be to you in your endeavours to progress in your profession or business. For Freddie this was the hypocrisy of it all. He found himself using the "facility" very little, since he couldn't stomach the hypocrisy. When he did make contact, it was more a case of the other person lining their own pockets.

What really hit home for Freddie was that when he was in trouble, he was provided with no support whatsoever, but asked merely to leave. Further still, it was his partner, Hammond, another Mason, who actually instigated all the trouble in the first place. The Masons made it very clear that they wanted no trouble there at the lodge and asked that both he and his partner leave. Of course, Freddie obstinately refused at first, since the situation had not been induced by him. Eventually however, he finally decided some time later, that he would be better off without them.

What had Freddie and his partner done to incite the Grand Provincial Master to make a decree against them?

13

The Fall of Atlas

The good times could not continue without a great deal of hard work and without the necessary finance, which was obviously achieved through hard work. Freddie was most definitely playing the field as far as his marriage was concerned, but he made sure this was not at the expense of his beloved Poseidon. Expansion of his company abroad, power and opportunity through the Magistrates and Freemasons, notoriety through his contact with politicians and stars – where could he go from here? Where could Poseidon go from here?

It is unfortunate that some businesses rise only through the merits and hard work of one partner. What happens when the other partner does not apply the same pressure? What happens when the other partner tries to take a free ride? Freddie could most definitely answer these questions for you. Freddie had been too involved. Too engrossed in expanding Poseidon and too involved in his affair with Helen to notice what was really going on. His return from a "business" trip abroad was to put him straight. Hammond, his partner was away on holiday and just for once Freddie felt it was time to acquaint himself with a little paper work. It wasn't something he normally touched; he felt that it wasn't really his forte. This was Hammond's job, he was good at it. Or so Freddie had thought! But what if something happened to Hammond, he'd have to get accustomed to paperwork then.

Freddie decided to surprise Hammond on his return from holiday, by clearing up some of the bills. That's when Freddie noticed a bill for bricks. Bricks, so what I hear you say – why not they were in business after all. But bricks were definitely not in their line of business. Freddie knew they had no extensions, no building work whatsoever. So, what were these bricks? Freddie decided to take this up with Hammond on his return. He didn't for a moment suspect anything unusual; he thought that perhaps he had just missed something important that he should be aware of. Hammond didn't even try to hide what was going on, he explained these bricks were, well, a sort of bonus for his hard work!

He even went so far as to suggest that Freddie do the same, why not he was working hard, Freddie should grant himself a bonus! Freddie just flipped. Cheating on your own company. This was like cheating on yourself. If you couldn't be true to yourself, who could you be true to? This was the road to bankruptcy Freddie explained. Hammond had to stop.

Freddie waited until the appropriate moment arrived when he could check out other areas of the business. He checked out the bought ledger very closely. He found bills there too. Scaffolding, architectural fees, cement, roofing tiles, structural surveys – there was no way these bills could be related to the company's purchasing requirements. No way at all! Freddie began to blame himself, for not being more diligent, for relying too much on someone else. What were these bills for? There was definitely no way that they could be put through the company books and in fact Freddie realised they would have had to be doctored – just for the sake of the books. The architects fees - £1,500 – down as reconstruction or movement of the walls in the warehouse. The bill would have to have been resubmitted by the architect himself. Freddie recognised the architect's name. He was none other than a fellow member of the Masonic lodge.

There was Freddie, worrying about trying to justify the amount of money they were making and all this time Hammond, his partner, had been justifying the money in a very different way. Hammond had been profiteering for his own ends; everything he had in life was financed by Poseidon. They were not justifiable expenses, but Hammond had been cunning, he realised that if you put them down as a business expense, they, the tax office that is, would look no further. Or, so he thought at the time! It would be to Freddie's cost not Hammond's, much later, when the tax people would really dig deep.

Hammond had even had the diabolical nerve to put his wife's medical bills through the company – she was after all the company secretary! Freddie's wife was a director – but he hadn't had anything for his wife. Freddie and Hammond were just Directors; Hammond had quite obviously thought there should also be substantial perks to this job. Hammond had moved to a larger house – as befitting his status of course. The Northern Staffs Scaffolding Company was an ideal company to provide the scaffolding for an extension and all the hardware required. The name was a huge coincidence, since a company already on Poseidon's books was one Northern Steel Stockholders, same initials, therefore possible confusion might just ensue. But by God, Hammond had been taking an awful risk and with Freddie's company.

One of the benefits, of course, of being a member of a Masonic Lodge, was that you could request certain favours from other members. Hammond had chosen to have the bills resubmitted and reworded, to fit in with necessary business requirements. Without the prior consent or approval of Freddie, Hammond had submitted private health care bills for his wife – and this, well this was just the tip of the iceberg. Freddie was infuriated, no that was too mild a word to use to explain the way that Freddie felt. This fraudulent bastard had put items through the company books without Freddie's knowledge. Freddie had financed the "business" trips, the holidays out of his own pocket, out of his own taxed income. There was no fraud involved. One of the major mistakes had been to trust his partner, to allow him to go unchecked.

Freddie confronted Hammond as soon as possible. Having got all the details clear in his mind and in his hand – he had the evidence, Hammond could deny nothing. Freddie made it clear, either he, Hammond should leave the company, or Freddie would go. Freddie wasn't going to support Hammond through his own hard work any longer. He would buy him out. In hindsight, what he should have done was to close the company down, in its entirety, bankrupt it, just like that! But hindsight unfortunately, is just that.

Freddie was determined to save his company, no matter what it cost. He rode on out to the company's bank at the time. You know the one with the black horse, the bank that likes to say yes. He spoke to the manager, explaining painfully that Hammond and he had had a difference of opinion, one that could not be resolved. Freddie realised that was stupid of him, he realised that now and he shouldn't have been so open. If anything, one thing he had learnt, was that you don't put all your cards on the table at once, especially with banks. Although this was as honest as he could make it at the time, it appeared there was some liability in having company partners who had a breakdown in communication. The bank didn't really want to have any upset, not where their money was concerned. And Freddie? Well, he was no longer prepared to support this money grabbing, lazy, little git.

So, the bank with its' black horse wouldn't help Freddie ride off into the sunset, now what? Freddie went to a different bank – the Midland bank. Well, as you would imagine, they welcomed him with open arms. They would, wouldn't they? They were prepared to jump in where other banks feared to tread. They were prepared to grant him funds for the company, continue to support the mortgage that they had on the property and they would also furnish him with £40,000 to buy Hammond out.

The next step was the solicitors. They acted a little like the bank with the black horse however, asking Freddie if he was really sure this was what he wanted, absolutely sure he could make it all work. What a question, when he, Freddie had been running the show most of the time anyway. Of course, he could make it all work. And so, the purchase of Hammond's shares in Poseidon went through, not without some difficulty however, since Hammond was a very embittered and acrimonious man. The loss of his illegitimate funds would put paid to his very lavish and very gracious lifestyle. Obviously, he had come to depend on these funds. Away he went however, with his tail between his legs, full of rage and revenge. But this was not the last Freddie was to hear of him, not by any stretch of an elastic imagination.

Poseidon carried on as usual, still expanding. Freddie working harder to make up for any possible loss of goodwill. Hammond in the meantime, had set up his own company before he left, called Chase Metals

Limited. His company lasted approximately twelve months, before going into liquidation and owing a lot of money to creditors. However, it appeared he, Hammond, had developed a new and significant talent – that of letter writing. Hammond had been writing allegedly anonymous letters, except that he forgot to disguise his writing. Freddie having known Hammond for many years knew instantly to whom the letters belonged. He was definitely not the sort of man to let go and he apparently intended to provide a great deal of hostility. No wonder his business failed, if this is how he spent his time.

Poseidon continued to expand still further, even better in fact, now they did not have the incredibly weighty ball and chain of Hammond around them. The biggest mistake Freddie was to make, unfortunately, was his hurry to get rid of Hammond. He should have let the company buy Hammond out, rather than he himself taking a stand, as a result he was left with the millstone of £40,000 around his neck, which he had to pay out of his own account. The only benefit to Freddie was the balance of the shares he obtained, all except two, of which Gabrielle owned.

Freddie had to return once more to Guernsey on business, purely business you understand. Although, you couldn't really expect him to go all alone, unaccompanied. Whilst he was away on the Friday night, the police called at his home. This was in fact not an unusual occurrence, since they would frequently request search warrants from him in his capacity as a Magistrate. On this occasion they called asking Gabrielle if Freddie was at home, to which she told them he was away on business. Gabrielle thought nothing of the matter up to this point, but then they requested the most unusual thing – they asked to gain admittance to the electricity meter which was in the garage. They took a cautious look at the meter, also carefully searching the garage with their eyes as they trundled through. Gabrielle advised them that he, Freddie would be back home on Saturday afternoon, to which they replied that they would return.

Freddie arrived home, tired and dishevelled from his journey, to find that his brother had been trying frantically to get in touch with him. The police apparently had been trying to contact him with regard to something other than the usual business. What was it they were after? Freddie couldn't imagine, but he didn't have long to wait. Gabrielle and Freddie were just sitting down to their evening meal with the boys, when there was knock on the door. Why, oh why, do people always arrive just as you are about to eat. However, the police were as good as their word, they had returned, with officers from the MEB. They explained that the MEB had received a report through an anonymous letter, that he had a black box on his electricity meter. To the uninitiated, this is a box which is fitted to the meter, which reverses the current.

Freddie was astounded to say the least. He couldn't comprehend what they were saying. It just didn't make sense. Here he was a wealthy business man, Magistrate, local disc jockey – a Lotus Esprit turbo parked on the drive, a house with a swimming pool, all the goodies, an income which could support those things and a fifty pound electricity bill each quarter. Ah-h.........well, of course, maybe that was it, fifty pounds a quarter was by no means excessive for an electricity bill, particularly not for a house the size of Breeme House. Perhaps that was what had attracted them to him? He could afford all the luxuries, because his bills were so small, therefore in their eyes he was obviously fiddling something. But the house was rarely used. In any case, he was a perfectionist, particularly when it came to being energy conscious.

They walked cautiously into the garage where they inspected the meter, first the MEB officers and then the Police. Of course, there was nothing there but the meter itself. Even though they had inspected it and found nothing, it did not mean to say that he was not guilty; he may have removed the box as far as they were concerned.

After all someone had reported the situation. That's when it hit Freddie, full force in the face. Of course someone had made a report and just who was it who had done this dastardly deed? The police said they were not at liberty to divulge the name of the person concerned. Freddie offered to quote some initials. What the heck, he had nothing to lose by guessing. He gave them John Hammond's initials, at which they confirmed he was right, but when he went on to quote the name of the person he suspected, this was where things differed. Freddie asked if he might see a copy of the letter. He knew straight away. No question about it. An alias may have been used, but there was no disguising Hammond's writing. They had been partners for far too long, far too many years.

The guess had paid off, but then Hammond was the only person he could think of who had such animosity towards him. Freddie explained the situation briefly to the police and the MEB, thinking that they would understand, thinking that they would believe him. Why, shouldn't they believe him – he was telling the truth after all. But of course, it could never be as simple as that.

The police went away. The MEB finally went

away. Both apparently satisfied that there was nothing untoward happening at Breeme House. But it couldn't stop there and Freddie couldn't let it rest there, even if he had wanted to. You see, it wasn't just a case of being cleared. The fact was that Freddie had been implicated in a crime, that of stealing electricity. As a Magistrate, pure implication was not permissible, even if Freddie managed to prove his innocence. All those who hold public office have to proceed on a point of order. Whether it was right or wrong, he would have to show, have proved that no dust had been swept under the carpet.

Freddie was summoned in due course to the Magistrates Court in Wolverhampton, from where the case was later sent to the Crown Court, since it was deemed to be difficult for one Magistrate to hear the case of another Magistrate. He awaited the development of the proceedings, but in the meantime of course was made to stand down not only as a Magistrate, but also as a radio presenter for Stour Valley Radio. Hammond knew how to hit below the belt all right, he had effectively done what no one so far in Freddie's life had been able to do. He had nipped his excessive energy in the bud. He knew the inactivity would kill Freddie, he knew that Freddie could not just sit around. At this particular point in time, Freddie could cheerfully have killed Hammond and there was nothing that he would not have done, in order to have got back at him, even stooping as low as Hammond himself.

For Freddie, everything stood still. A bounding, black cloud appeared over the horizon. For the first time ever, Freddie did not know what to do. He had been falsely charged with obtaining electricity by theft. He was unable to do the things he loved and worse still he was a Freemason in a lodge with the same person who had sent this poison pen letter. The only good thing of course, was that Hammond hadn't the guts to show up at the lodge when he knew that Freddie was there. On the other hand, perhaps it was a good idea, since Freddie would have loved to have got his hands on him, given half a chance. In fact, he probably couldn't have trusted himself had Hammond turned up at the same time as he was there. The hate, the animosity which welled up inside of Freddie as a result of the lies Hammond had told was indescribable.

The Freemasons of course, obviously got wind of the ill feeling between Hammond and himself. They began by suspending Hammond and asking Freddie to refrain from attending until the matter was resolved. If you think that was bad enough for Freddie, then to add insult to injury, they had also asked him to pay the year's subscription for the period he wasn't allowed to attend. What crass hypocrisy.

They couldn't make a decision for themselves. They could only sit on the fence and await the outcome. They would await the winner, the strongest contender, right or wrong, then they would fall in behind that person. They weren't prepared to back anybody, even though Freddie had evidence, the proof of his innocence.

Freddie looked at his bank balance. He looked at the assets which he had – which were really quite substantial at this point in time. He tried to look at things from a logical point of view. Even though he was having to go through what amounted to a show trial for a Magistrate, just to clear his name. Nevertheless, this Greek God, this James Bond, couldn't stand the pace; he couldn't suffer the persistence of the newspapers chasing him for a story. At first it was "JP ACCUSED OF THEFT" but the case dragged on so long, it followed other aspects of his life too such as "JP ATTEMPTS TO COMMIT HARI KARI IN PLANE CRASH".

He tried to put it all into perspective. If he had really been going to pull off a scam, it would have been for a far greater amount than a piffling little sum of twenty to thirty pounds a quarter. He had a lot to lose and it wasn't worth that amount of money. Apart from the logistics of things, such a small amount of money would not have been his style. He would maybe have robbed a train for a quarter of a million pounds, jumped on a boat and joined Ronnie Biggs. But theft wasn't his style. Hard work, showmanship, the gift of the gab, even a little of the conman in him, but very definitely nothing malicious. Besides if being a Freemason had taught him nothing else, then it had taught him always "to be cautious!"

One of the things that very obviously played a part in the proceedings at this point was without doubt jealousy. Here he was, a young man, a Magistrate, a radio presenter, a Lotus Esprit Turbo in the garage, wearing handmade tailored suits, and living in a nice house with a swimming pool – who could blame them? One of the officers, in fact PC Cockburn, subsequently renamed much later by Freddie as "cock-up" for reasons which will not be expanded upon here, was heard to have said.

"This one could do with a comeuppance!"

They all took an instant dislike to Freddie, because of his situation. Although situation probably isn't quite the right word, more a case of his position, or ability to make money and create power. So their jealousy was quite understandable really. Not condonable, but very understandable. They had no idea of his background, his financial circumstances, his income, or anything else about him – but he was a suspect all the same. Such a young man could not have achieved all this, in his short life span, without it being ill gotten gains. He'd had a similar effect on the two officers from the MEB, who gave an assessment of what his electricity usage was likely to have been in a home of this size and status. They estimated it should have been somewhere around £170 to £220 per quarter. In fact, Freddie was made aware through his own close, personal contacts, that jealousy had affected the perusal of the case. Instructions had been given at one point by a reviewing officer, to abandon the case due to lack of evidence – all they had was the letter. However, the case was to be pursued, purely as a result of personal animosity and ill feeling.

Freddie was going spare. The James Bond of Wombourne couldn't take all this subterfuge. He needed something to take his mind off things. What could he do? He had held a position of trust as a Magistrate. If by any chance and it was only a chance, he should be found guilty, through a twist of evidence against him, would he go inside? Even with no previous record. These thoughts churned around in his mind, even though he knew justice had to prevail, there was no evidence and he was not guilty!

But the thoughts still crept in where they weren't wanted, locking away his ability to think clearly and logically, throwing away the key to his senses. He threw himself into his work, even more so than before. Then he'd sit back, reflect and look upon his life. God, what a mess! He would pay anything to clear his name. He hired one of the best lawyers in Birmingham. He had hired the best barrister. He hired the best forensic analyst Birmingham could offer. To crown it all, the MEB even had the cheek to charge him £200 for a replacement meter. Nevertheless, he was determined to prove that he wasn't the seedy little wheeler dealer they portrayed him as.

Both Helen and Gabrielle were swanning around in the background, there to help him when needed, there to support him if he should fall. But it was to Gabrielle to whom he turned. He needed something to take his mind off things. It was Gabrielle he turned to for advice. She wasn't just a wife, she was a friend too. What could he do that he hadn't already done, to take his mind off his problems? He was fighting fit and proud of it, up until now that is. Not a multi muscle Atlas of a man – just fit. He enjoyed swimming, diving, skiing, tennis, squash, clay pigeon shooting, fast cars, fast business and fast ladies! But he still had too much time on his hands, too much time that allowed him to think of what might loom ahead. He contemplated parachuting; he had always wanted to jump from a plane. Who knows, perhaps it would bring him down to earth a little. But no, Gabrielle, as much as she may have hated him at the time for his illicit affair with Helen, didn't want him tackling anything that might be dangerous. The last thing she wanted was a dead, unfaithful husband.

Freddie began to hang around the local airport at Bobbington whenever he had some spare time, purely out of curiosity at first. Flying seemed to suggest freedom, both from his thoughts and from his problems. He wished he could just jump on a plane right there, right then and take off for some paradise isle – blue sky, blue sea, plenty of sun, sand and sex. Then his thoughts wandered back to Helen, would she go with him? Would he really have the nerve to leave Gabrielle and the boys? Could he do that? Would it really be fair? Particularly after all that had happened. His thoughts raced ahead, mind in turmoil. Funnily enough, when he made his decision, it was to Gabrielle that he turned for agreement, for backing. He decided to take up flying; it was something he felt that would honestly take his mind off his problems. Something that was new, something that was exciting and something which suggested for Freddie at least, the continuance of his playboy lifestyle.

Having approached the local flying school and having taken his medical and passed with flying colours, he was ready to go. The first hour's instruction was like a dream come true. Taxiing along the runway, then away you go at seventy to eighty miles an hour, full flaps, rotate and you're away. It wasn't a bit like taking off in a 747 to Ibiza or some other holiday destination. He was up there in the cockpit, able to see for miles around and down!

This had just been a practice run and needless to say he signed up for another ten lessons. By the fourth lesson he was ready to take far more control. Ken, the instructor, insisted that Freddie was now ready to take the pilot's seat and to issue more firm commands. The first of these commands was to radio to the control tower at Bobbington.

"Golf, Alpha, Tango, Uniform, Charlie (this was the sign of the aircraft) requests permission to taxi and assume takeoff position."

Freddie was given permission to go ahead; he heard his words repeated back to him by the air traffic controller but with the addition that he may take off at his discretion. Jesus he felt great, he was the guy in charge of the next space launch! Well, that's the way it felt at the time. Full thrust, brakes off, down flaps, pull back on the hand control and you're away. Climbing steadily first to 1,500 feet, you concentrate so much at this stage, you think of little else. Slow curve to the left and then up to 3,000 feet. You're at the final stage. The world is your oyster. You can see for miles around. On a clear day you feel like God, able to watch all from above. But it was only an exercise on this occasion and what goes up must come down and that was a different task.

Coming down through the paces once more, Freddie radioed in to say that he was ready to land. He was given the all clear, but was told that he was number three. On hell! Number three! That was the last thing he wanted. This meant he had to spot the other two planes in front of him and taxi in on the arse of number two on the final approach. He immediately looked to the left, following the flight path of the circuit. Fortunately for Freddie on this occasion, the runway was just taking down a Cessna that was number one. Now he had to find number two. He traced the circuit back in his view, went up for the final approach of the one that had just landed. Where the hell was number two? He wasn't in view. He wasn't on the final leg! Freddie looked across and urgently spotted him. Another Cessna. Thank Christ for that! Beads of perspiration ran down Freddie's face as relief set in.

Finally, it was Freddie's turn. On his final approach, he radioed in to report his position. Down to 1,000 feet, then over the trees, clear the hedges, runway in front.

Down, down still further, watching the altimeter, checking the speed, undercarriage down and fixed, 800 feet! 400 feet! Down with the power, 100 feet........ That's when your vision of the runway disappears. You fly the plane by your guts, the wind coming underneath the belly of the plane. The final, gentle bump. Brakes locked on. Then slowly, slowly, taxiing back to the hanger. Lesson over. Exhilaration in place. This was better than having sex. Yes, it definitely was!

Several more flying experiences; then came the exam,

the oral and the written exam in the office. The examiner Ali arrived to check the aircraft, the tyres, the fuel, the brakes, the linkages and the exterior of the plane. He wondered if Ali would ask him to do an emergency stop, after all this was more rigorous than a driving test!

"Right then off you go" Ali commanded.

"My instructor isn't here yet" Freddie explained.

No instructor necessary." Ali said. "You're going solo!"

Jesus, was he serious? Yes, very serious. This was the examination to test Freddie's ability to fly solo and no he couldn't have another lesson first. Ali ordered Freddie into the plane. Someone else was actually giving the orders for a change. Freddie checked the seriousness of Ali's tone; this was no mean man to mess about with. He did just as he was instructed; he clambered into the cockpit, just as he had on other occasions, but this time alone.

He was frightened. He was gobsmacked to say the least. This man of metal, of unadulterated steel, was scared stiff. He sat, checked out the instruments, checked the radio and gave one clear shout to warn anyone standing near before he started up the plane. Permission to taxi, take off and away. The start of the engine matched his heart beat; the vibration of each went simultaneously together. Most people with a little bit of knowledge, can take an aircraft off the ground, but landing one was a different concept. All these things were going through his mind, a little like a computer on overdrive. No crowds, nothing special, no people lining the runway to see Freddie Jones fly in, just an examiner waiting to give his appraisal. It had been a perfect landing and surprise, surprise, for Freddie anyway, he passed, one would almost say with "flying" colours.

Another surprise waited in store for Freddie however, Gabrielle had had the feeling that she must go to the airport that day. She brought the boys with her and there they were as he landed the plane. Superhero Freddie! Superhero Dad! A wonderful job. They milled around him, exulting in this special moment with him. He didn't need the examiner to tell him that he had passed, just having them there, seeing the praise in their eyes was enough, enough for Freddie.

Hero! It didn't give him any exemption from the court case he was facing. It didn't solve his problems at all. A fully fledged pilot he may be, but when he came down to the ground the problems were still there. In any case, he needed more flying experience, particularly if he was to fly for long distances, through cloud or at night. He still wasn't free. He still couldn't do exactly as he wanted.

If he was going to take the plane further, higher, through thick and thin, then he had to have his IMC rating. More hours flying on Saturday, during the week, going out on Tuesday, getting a couple of hours in here and there. It was a matter of getting his log filled in up to date. All this had to be carried out without Helen knowing. She didn't like him flying. In fact, it was rather peculiar, she had actually said at one point that she had had a premonition of some disaster. She frequently said she was a witch, that she had the ability to foresee the future. Helen didn't like him flying, so he now had to make excuses to her to keep her in blissful ignorance of what he was doing. After all, it was there to help him forget his problems.

It was at this point in time that Helen decided to tell Phil, her husband, of her relationship with Freddie. His first reaction apparently was to go and "beat the living daylights" out of Freddie, even though it had been his suggestion, a few years previously. It had been his suggestion, just before and after they were married, that had started all the fiasco in the first place. It was this that had pushed Helen and Freddie together. She told Phil clearly and plainly, that she had gone ahead with his suggestion, she had tried it on with Freddie, initially just for a lark, but that finally she liked what she saw. She had in fact been a little bit like a female Julius Caesar – "she came, she saw, she conquered" – possibly even in that order. Freddie also thought of her openness, when she mentioned she had told Phil of their relationship. He supposed that this would result in her also telling Phil all that they had experienced together, all that they had been through. She would probably even go on to explain how they had even committed adultery in the sacred marital bed. Phil must have resolved that it was a useless situation and remarkably gave her an uncontested divorce. Very quiet, very quick, very private. Purely a quiet dissolution of the marriage.

This was trouble that Freddie could well have done without at this point in time, it would only add further to his problems. However, what was done was done and now Gabrielle must be told also. Gabrielle had to be told clearly what was going on, before other more malicious tongues could wag. Freddie told her that he had found someone else, someone he loved beyond life itself. Up to this point Gabrielle had only had an inkling that something was going on. She wasn't quite sure what and she had no evidence – not concrete anyway. Now though, she had it straight from the horse's mouth. He didn't know quite what to expect, but he felt the hurt. Gabrielle recoiled in horror, as if she had been stabbed. She appeared to recede into a shell for sometime afterwards, as if to make the hurt go away.

But life must go on and of course for Helen and Freddie, it did. Nothing had changed for them, except that now everything was out in the open. No more deception. No more creeping about. No more James Bond. Perhaps this was when things began to lose their zest. Perhaps this is when it began to turn sour.

Of course, Helen still didn't like him flying. The result was more lies and cover ups but with Helen this time, instead of Gabrielle. He had just removed the secrecy from one partner to another. A different format maybe, but secrecy just the same. So the Jekyll and Hyde character continued, with Freddie telling Helen he was going on business, when all the time he was flying. Perhaps now Helen was having the suspicions that Gabrielle had been having previously. But he loved flying, by this time it was everything to him. Perhaps on reflection, this is why he finally stayed with Gabrielle; she allowed his spirit to roam free.

In fact, flying consumed him at the time, since it continued to help him forget his pending legal problems.

Helen bought a maisonette, a town house in Amblecote. This, she hoped would enable Freddie and her to have more freedom, to spend more time together. Freddie helped out where he could, purchasing items of furniture and paying the legal fees. Freddie felt that as Helen was becoming so much a part of his life, that it would be better if she didn't work so closely with him. He wanted the company to run like clockwork. He wanted no animosity to allow people to say that she got things because................ And he wanted the relationship between himself and Helen to remain the same.

He suggested to Helen, that as they would quite possibly be an item shortly she should move to another company, where she wasn't under his immediate control. It would give her outside contacts, a different range of skills, greater experience; it was all going to be better for her in the end. After all, she had been with him since her school leaving days; it would help her to be a little more independent of him. This didn't go down very well with Helen, but she could see his point. Or could she?

So Helen moved on and joined a computer company in Halesowen. Freddie bought her a car, gave her an expense account and a credit card, all of which she could charge her petrol and her car to. He gave her a little independence from him. Freddie travelled frequently to Halesowen in the lunch hour to spend time with Helen, allowing his company to run itself for a while, hell it was time the company paid him back a little.

On April 2nd 1988 at 8.30am, a crisp, cool bright morning, Freddie clambered aboard his aircraft at Bobbington Airport. He was there to take his IMC rating having put in sufficient hours to upgrade his standards. With Ken Turner as commander of the aircraft, they took off going through the normal procedure and traversed up to the first circuit. They were going on a pre-programmed flight. Freddie knew Helen was at Borth in Wales and it was at this point that he mentioned to Ken that she was there on holiday for a few days with her sister. Freddie knew Ken quite well by this time, they had been good friends. Ken was a lively guy, very broad minded. Freddie asked Ken if there was any way they could fly to Borth, straight on to the beach. He felt daring. He felt secure. The objective was to leave Freddie at Borth, although Ken said that he would come back and pick Freddie up. All the time Freddie was thinking "Who knows, maybe today's the day, perhaps now I should make that move".

It was a cold morning, made sharp by a little frost. A mist hung around, with sharp spears of sunlight attacking the ground. Freddie had parked his XJS in the private car park at the airport, used by aircraft owners and pilots. High up there amongst the rays, he could forget about worldly possessions. They rose still further, rising up over the Long Mynd, the range of hills in Shropshire. At this point Ken asked Freddie to take over the controls, not an unusual request in itself, but at this particular stage Freddie thought it odd. Still, he thought "Yeah, okay". Freddie took the controls and as he did so he felt the stiffness in them and explained the situation to Ken through his intercom. Ken nodded in agreement stating that he thought they had frozen up. A cold reptile chill slithered up Freddie's spine, what did Ken mean, they had frozen up. Was this also part of the test, was Ken waiting for a reaction or suggestion? No, Freddie had felt the controls himself, there was no way this was a jest on Ken's part.

Everything was frozen solid; they had no elevation, no ascension, nothing at all.

The engine started to make the noise that you really don't want to hear flying at any height. The engine was not firing correctly; it was literally missing, a little like a car with petrol that's too rich. Neither Ken nor Freddie spoke. There was nothing to say. There was no panic. Just fear! Ken continued to try to get the engine to fire properly – no good, it just wasn't having it. Freddie was doing the best he could, in an inexperienced sort of way. Freddie had never been really very religious, but he began to pray now, to pray that Ken could get them out of this situation. The screen began to frost over. Before long they had no vision, the frost producing heavy patterns over the screen. Freddie could see from the altimeter that they were losing height.

Then the terrible sound came – no sound at all! The engine had stopped. They were on collision course with whatever was in front of them. They were now in destiny's hands. Still nothing was said. Nothing could be said. Ken hit the engine start button again to try to get the engines running. Nothing! Nothing at all! Then the sound that broke the silence, the SOS MAYDAY. They were only likely to be intermittent on the radar screens of control towers, because of travelling between the mountains. They knew this was the end!

14

The Fall of Atlantis

Black! Black! Everything was black! He tried with enormous strength to have some vision – any vision. He was dead! He must be dead! Or was he? No one could really tell. Freddie couldn't tell. For Freddie it had seemed like an eternity, reaching what appeared to be their final destination, their final impact. It had been like the proverbial nightmare. Shadows fleeing past the aircraft window. An horrendous crashing noise, like a herd of elephants, storming through a jungle. His body, like the plane breaking into a thousand tiny pieces, or so it felt. He must be dead. He had to be dead. He couldn't feel a thing and everything was blacker than night.

Later, much later, when he came around in hospital – no much later than that even – he was to realise just how lucky he had been. Freddie's aircraft seat had shot forward on impact, with Freddie still harnessed inside. Freddie, well, he hit the flight deck, the gyroscope tearing off his nose, ripping out his eye and gouging out all the flesh on the right side of his cheek. His jaw and left ankle each smashed in four places and worst of all his spine had broken in two places. Had he been swimming, or even diving at the time, you would have likened him to nothing more than a jelly fish, looking at his shape.

He sat slumped in a heap. The former James Bond, was in a heap on a deserted hillside, in an aircraft which no longer resembled an aircraft and which was about to explode.

It was also much later, when on the road to recovery that Freddie was made aware that he had to give thanks to several very special people. To the farmers who had found him and reacted so quickly, to John Sankey, Stan Bloor and Dave Allen, medical men extraordinaire and to Mr Olley, the consultant at Shrewsbury Hospital, who painstakingly pieced Freddie back together again. To all of these, he owed a debt he could never repay.

It was to Mr Olley that Freddie would turn in times of pain, in times of stress and in times of mental fatigue. At times it was purely that, mental fatigue, a formulated sense of madness, his mind not always knowing what was going on, but also not knowing who he was. In fact, madness didn't go nearly far enough to describe the state he was in at times. Frequently under sedation for the constant pain he was in, he would have dreams, which could be better described as hallucinations. In his hospital room, the view on the wall opposite his bed was that of a scenic sea panorama. Freddie firmly believed for some time, that he was by the side of the sea, even at times imagining the sound of the waves. Another time he dreamt that he had met Robert Maxwell and had bought half the shares in the Mirror Group of newspapers, then the next morning he went on to remonstrate with the newspaper lady, he didn't see why he should pay for the newspaper, since he owned half of the shares. He even went on to discuss the payment of £5million with his accountant in payment of the shares.

His family had rallied around him. Gathering to generate a generous gilding of love, warmth and affection, in the hope of healing his wounds. Both Gabrielle and Helen travelled to see Freddie as often as they could,

Gabrielle, in fact, visiting him every single day. Both at the same time? Well, no of course not! Whilst they were very much aware of each other, they had no desire to cross paths, in fact if anything, they probably blamed each other for the accident of the man they loved.

Why didn't Helen come every day? Well by this time she was eight and a half months pregnant and travelling to Shrewsbury and back and the worry of Freddie wasn't doing her a lot of good.

Helen visited Freddie in hospital, always ensuring first of all that his family were not by his side. However many of the patients were in a similar mental state to Freddie and frequently found it difficult to reason situations. On one occasion, the guy in the next bed made what could have been a fatal mistake. Whilst Gabrielle was sitting one day by Freddie's bedside, in general conversation with him, the gentleman in the next bed enquired how the baby was. Well, what could Freddie say? What could he do? Whilst Freddie's family was aware of Helen they were not aware of her state of play. Fairly remarkable really, when, you consider the size of her at this time. Well, Freddie may have been ill, but his mind was just as active. In his usual style, he laughed it off, mentioning that the man wasn't quite himself.

On another occasion, whilst walking to the ward through the hospital to visit Freddie, she had spotted a couple who she knew were close friends of both Freddie and Gabrielle. She dived for cover, but too late. Peter, the husband later remarked to Freddie, that he was sure he had seen Freddie's secretary outside and that she was very heavily pregnant. He even went on to refer to the fact that he had thought she had split up from her husband, but of course it was just possible that they had reconciled – wasn't it?

Suddenly, Helen no longer came. What had happened? Why didn't she come? Had she decided that she could no longer stand the look of him? He was soon to find out. A telephone call was to put him out of his misery, explaining that Helen had been taken into labour and was presently in Wordsley Hospital. A boy. She had had a boy. This fine young perfect baby boy, she named Luke Frederic John. Luke Freddie believed after the chapel of St Luke at the hospital in Oswestry. Frederic after himself and John after her own father.

It would have been such an easy get out. For three whole weeks, whilst Freddie had been in a coma, he had had no dreams, just a black void. Well as far as he could remember anyway. When he came out of the coma, well, he still couldn't remember anything – not even his £42,000 XJS. It came in fact as a massive surprise to Freddie that he had such a car in the first place. By his bedside when he came around, had been his brother and of course Gabrielle. The next day Helen had sneaked in to let him know she was by his side and still thinking of him. Yes, he knew who they were, but it would have been so easy for him to have said that he didn't know them at all.

One thing that could always be said for Freddie was that he had – has – the constant ability to smile through adversity. When the worst comes to the worst Freddie still goes on smiling. Even at his worst, whilst still in the hospital, Freddie could always see the funny side of things. On one occasion Mr Brown, the eye specialist came to see him. Now bearing in mind that Freddie had lost the sight in his right eye, this was not unusual. Mr Brown, an excellent specialist, obviously felt it was unwise to inform Freddie of all the facts and for some weeks actually failed to tell Freddie that he had lost that eye. However, Mr Brown paid a visit to Freddie one day and pointed out

"Now, Mr Jones, we are going to fit you with a prosthesis, a glass eye basically. It will move up, down, left and right. It will be exactly the same colour as your other eye, identical in fact in every detail, other than the fact that you can't see through it.

Well due to the fact that Freddie was a little around the bend at the time anyway, but also due to the fact that he liked to take the Mickey out of himself for having lost his nose and eye, he instantly replied,

"Well if I can't see through it, it won't be a lot of use. Why don't you just drill a hole in it, then I'll be able to see through it."

Mr Brown just raised his eyebrows and walked away. In all probability he had heard this joke before. But perhaps he didn't "see" the joke, or latch on to Freddie's sick sense of humour at this time.

Freddie was in fact, always trying to take the piss out of himself. Like the time he ended up with his own bodily fluids tipped all over him. As a paraplegic – paralysed from the waist down – he like many others lost all lavatorial functions. There was just no control over his waterworks. He was catheterised and given a bottle. At night nurses would come and turn him every hour so that he didn't get pressure sores. However, in order to do this they had to remove the bottle from the bed. Having turned him, he asked for the bottle to be returned. Unfortunately for Freddie, on this one occasion, they hadn't noticed which way out the bottle had been taken, or in fact, which way back it was being put and unfortunately they gave it back neck downwards. The bottle having already been used was in no fit state to be rotated as if in a milk churn and as a consequence poor Freddie and his bed were soaked. As Freddie said at the time

"Look take the piss out of me during the day if you want to, but I do enjoy my sleep."

The nurses, of course at around 3 o clock in the morning were busy cleaning both Freddie and his bed.

Well, Freddie finally came out of hospital. Not fighting fit of course, but in a wheelchair, paralysed from the waist down. The top half was okay albeit that he needed a lot of cosmetic surgery on his face. But below the waist – well that was a different matter; they had told him at the hospital that as a paraplegic, he would not be able to get an erection. At first, he was well, just a little mortified. What man wouldn't be! However, he knew from the start that they were wrong, he had these feelings, these sensations and he just knew that they were wrong. Then of course there was the other factor. Well, he hadn't worked in the metal trade for all these years without some advantage. When you have steel piping, anyone in the metal trade will tell you, you have to have an erection.

He went to a meeting at the hospital to hear about the pros and cons, the benefits and drawbacks of being paralysed. Perhaps things weren't quite as bad as they appeared, or were they? Not long after his discharge, the letter telling him of the date for the Crown Court hearing date for his alleged electricity fraud landed on his doormat.

Everything that had happened to Freddie, all his problems, his broken back, his disfigurement, all these had been caused by his attempt to get away from being persecuted for something he hadn't done. He needed now to sit back, take stock, analyse his life and at some time look for the reward. There always had to be a reward.

The reward was in fact to be a long time coming. While Freddie was attempting to get back on his feet, something which the hospital said that he would never do, The Crown Prosecution Service attempted to strike a deal with him. They suggested that if he resigned as a Magistrate, they would drop the charges against him for allegedly stealing electricity. Freddie was having none of this. He was not going to be associated with a criminal act. It was as simple as that. HE WAS NOT GUILTY!

A reward there had to be! But definitely not at this point in time. They say that good luck or bad luck runs in threes, well Freddie's luck was running into millions – and that wasn't just events. Freddie remembered the previous events well. Almost the sort of memories you have for good times, very memorable, except they weren't, not by any stretch of the imagination. When Freddie had been called before the Magistrates Court prior to his accident, the television and press had made a field day of it. They were obviously very interested in this Magistrate, who was currently in front of a Magistrates Court, basically for theft of electricity from the MEB. They probably thought that this was the sort of thing you found in the "have nots", but definitely not from someone of his standing, a man who appeared to be loaded with money. This made it even more interesting for the newspapers. With Freddie's experience on the bench, he knew that this was going to be the case. He came prepared.

On the first occasion he pulled up in his Lotus Esprit turbo and onto the car park underneath the Council buildings, which are opposite the Magistrates Court in Wolverhampton. Spotting the camera crews from TV and the newspaper reporters queuing up at the bottom of the steps, which led up to the Court, he donned his disguise. A theatrical moustache and beard, a pair of glasses and a Dirk Bogarde style hat, an old overcoat and a walking stick. He then proceeded to walk, no limp, across the car park, past the reporters and past the television crews, none of whom took any notice of him. Hell, they were looking for someone by the name of Frederic Jones and this didn't look a bit like him. He walked up the steps to the Court, into the robing room with his solicitor and removed his disguise. Replacing the disguise on the way out, the newspaper men must have realised that they had been duped.

On the next occasion he decided to go one better, he knew that they would be looking for his car, so he borrowed a motor bike and leathers from a close friend. All these were donned over the smart suit that he had worn for his court appearance. He walked past the reporters even passed the detective sergeant who was handling his case and he didn't recognise him. They obviously thought he was a biker in for some speeding or motoring offence. These were two of the most successful illusions he had ever created. The next time he was to attend the Court would be after the crash and he would be in a wheelchair. A perfect disguise!

It was most definitely time for a reward. Back on his feet, a little, he began to feel the loss of Helen. Since he had been stuck at home all day, they had been very much incommunicado and of course his beautiful Poseidon had not fared too well either. He had to get back to work and back to his usual routine. He would have none of this nonsense about not walking again. And so........his first task was to go on holiday. He booked a holiday to Madeira, the Hotel Savoy no less, with the lady Helen and the new baby. How did Gabrielle feel? Well she was certainly hurt especially after what she had gone through on behalf of Freddie. But in her wisdom she decided to let the rope run free, just holding it gently, until the time came to give it a tug.

Here was the playboy, the married playboy, who had everything. Here was the playboy taking his mistress on holiday to Madeira, an utterly fabulous island and the people warm and friendly – not "money grabbing friendly" as some had appeared in the past. They appeared to accept Freddie for what he was and for what he looked like. Did he say playboy? They were of course shown to a fabulous suite, the Chantal suite, but things were never actually going to be the same again, they couldn't could they? I mean to say, he really was no longer the happy go lucky playboy and she his mistress. It was more a case of the disfigured playboy and his mistress - plus baby! The situation wasn't the same; the characters weren't even the same. Nevertheless, he wasn't going to be put off, not our Freddie. Even with his disability he was going to try to give a damn good show.

On Madeira the weather was fantastic. It was extremely warm – allowing Helen to portray her still beautiful figure, even after having a baby. It was indeed semi-tropical, with clear blue skies and the countryside was sheer fantasy. Beautiful blooms of all varieties and colours, the vegetation also consisted of pomegranates and grapes. Hiring a car and a driver, they were taken to see all the sights around the coast and in the mountains, everywhere in fact worth seeing. From the window of their suite they could see the ship the Black Prince lying in port, all its sails billowing in the breeze.

In Madeira they love children, so it was not surprising that Helen and Freddie got on particularly well with the locals, they did after all have Luke with them. However, it was brought home to them that they were no longer on their own. They did not have the intimacy of two people in love. The Garden of Eden with Adam and Eve had now been infiltrated by another person. Things were truly never going to be the same again. Perhaps this would be the end of the story. Stop while the going was good. But life isn't like that is it?

The fortnight was amazing, the island beautiful, the food, hotel, company – all fantastic. The island itself was restful and invigorating. But for Helen it most definitely wasn't the same. She was now with someone who was disabled, who wasn't quite the fit to do everything, go everywhere person that she used to travel with. Helen now had the restrictions placed upon her by a disabled guy and a young baby. Perhaps this was the king pin that put the death knell in their relationship. There was most definitely something missing.

Reward? It was more like a booby prize. Helen and Freddie arrived home, back to Birmingham to the start of two legal cases. The Crown Court appearance and also the personal injury case for the compensation for the accident were both looming on the horizon. Freddie appeared in court for the criminal case, taking his place in the dock in a wheelchair. Asked how he pleaded, he knew well what to say, he had rehearsed this one line so often. The Judge in fact decided that the prosecution had insufficient evidence, since the case had been brought purely on the basis of the letter received from Freddie's former partner John Hammond, but under an assumed name. The Judge directed the jury to enter a not guilty verdict. At last – cleared. Not that it felt that way. The newspapers in their normal course reported "JP CLEARED OF THEFT" but in much smaller print than before. Nothing like the spread that he had been given in the beginning, when they had thought that he was guilty. So to the public possibly, he was just as guilty as ever.

Having been cleared meant that Freddie would be awarded his legal costs from public funds and Freddie could sue the arse off John Hammond. The Judge in fact, made a point of saying, that the whole case had been motivated by the horrendous animosity of his former business partner.

He, the Judge, went on to point out that the case should not have been brought to court in the first place. Freddie of course, left court with his head held high – albeit four feet high sat in a wheelchair.

It was time to go away on holiday again. This time to Marbella. Not much of a holiday for sunbathing and the beach. After all, Freddie could no longer fit into his swimming trunks. His left leg was wasted due to the nerves that were connected to the spine dying. Freddie's left leg was in fact a third of the normal size. However, this didn't stop Helen showing off her ample charms once more. They visited places that had meant so much to both of them on previous occasions. They visited Toni Dali's, where the accordionist, once more played the songs that he had played before. If ever there was a "play it again Sam" moment this was it. They visited all the places that brought back the memories. It was like a joy ride, like an attempt to grasp at something that was slipping from your fingers, it was full of reminiscences. Freddie, well he was there in the contentment that tonight, this princess, the one that everyone was looking at, she was going to bed with him.

Some may say Freddie had his head screwed on all right – keeping a wife and family at home and taking a mistress on holiday – but most of those who were close to him knew that his state of mind obviously was not secure.

Freddie arrived home from their holiday having made two very distinct decisions. First, he would exchange his current XJS – a major decision! To Freddie however it was important, albeit whether he was mad or not, to keep up appearances and who wouldn't appear in a £47,000 XJS 5.3 litre convertible, with tinted windows, leather seats and air conditioning. His second decision was to take out a libel action against John Hammond; he was going to take him for everything that he had. As it happened, when the case came to court, Freddie won. Well, who thought he wouldn't? However, Hammond actually had the nerve to appeal. Freddie won. Hammond appealed again, once again Freddie won. Over a period of three years Freddie constantly fought Hammond in the courts, always funding his action by making use of the compensation from his aircraft accident. It came to light in the final appeal, that it was actually due to the incompetence of Hammond's own solicitor in Dudley, that there had been a need for the three sets of hearings in the first place.

Everyone was aware that Freddie was in a sense mentally unstable. The solicitors were under no misapprehension, since Freddie had settled for the meagre amount of £77,000 as compensation for his injuries. It was only on reflection now, that he realised that this sum was nowhere near the amount he should have received for his injuries. In fact, if he had taken it to the High Court there was every likelihood that he would have been awarded somewhere in the region of £750,000 to £1 million, so his solicitors informed him. But because he was a little crazy, £77,000 seemed an awful lot of money to him at the time. However, although Freddie was awarded his costs back from the Hammond escapade, he was financially in a difficult position. He could afford to fund law cases against Hammond, or anyone else for that matter no longer.

The court cases against Hammond and also that for the compensation for the accident had taken more than three years. These facts along with Freddie's injuries were bound to take their toll on his health, on his relationships and on his business. Rewards were to be few and far between and now on reflection Freddie felt that these factors had all contributed towards the downfall of relationships and his beloved Poseidon. It was possible to see now, that he could not give satisfactory attention to all, without something losing out.

Initially, to add insult to injury, whilst Freddie had been more than fair in being forthright with the Inland Revenue after he bought Hammond out, he learnt that truthfulness was not always the best policy.

As they say "crime pays", or so it appeared. The Inland Revenue went to see Freddie with regard to Hammond's false accounting within the company, he was more than helpful to them, bearing in mind that Hammond had had more than his fair share of the company. Freddie in fact, was so overwhelmed that someone would actually be there to agree with him, which they did. Freddie handed over all the information, including that based on the fraud of the company, including such facts as the use of funds for extensions to Hammond's house and the private health care for his wife. What more could he do? He had bent over backwards to supply them with as much information as possible.

The bombshell was yet to drop. The Inland Revenue were going to charge Freddie the tax which the company as liable for, which Hammond had escaped due to the fact that Freddie had purchased Hammond's shares in the company. Unfortunately for Freddie, there is a law which says that if you buy someone's shares, you also buy their liabilities, for the period of time for which they owned those shares. Freddie was liable for some £30,000, this was money he had received in compensation for the plane crash, which he had put into the company to help it to trade and continue to expand. Now, after all the struggling, he had to pay the money to the vultures, to the organisation he had thought would be on his side against Hammond.

He thought back to the time when he had been on a business trip with Hammond. They were travelling between the mill of Acerinox in Madrid and their Head Office. On the day that Freddie had been about to fly out from Malaga to Madrid, Hammond had decided that he would rather play golf on the Rio Real golf course in Malaga. This in itself had angered Freddie, since business always came first.

The event was made worse by the fact that after one lunchtime bingeing session, Hammond had actually come at Freddie with a knife. Freddie was walking away from him at the time and he was making his way down some rather steep steps. Hammond unfortunately took two steps down from the top and in his drunken state, fell down the rest. The knife fortunately went one way and Hammond went the other. Mike Newbrook, another colleague, who had made the journey with them, was required to look after Hammond, whilst Freddie went off to Madrid to conclude the business with Acerinox. Freddie felt that strictly speaking, Hammond was without a doubt the traditional British lager lout.

What with Hammond's foolishness, the court case

for the alleged electricity fraud, the tax man clamouring for money, which Hammond had personally used, his horrific injuries due to the plane crash and the pain which went with that and Helen's rejection – was it any wonder that Poseidon was to be affected.

Freddie could cope no longer. It was all a little too much. He couldn't give the time that was required to keep his business going, let alone build it up. He was too busy fighting everyone and everything. Maybe this should be a lesson to us all – "take care of the things that mean the most."

During this crazy period, when Freddie had struggled to keep everything going, including his battles, three companies had gone into liquidation owing Poseidon some £55,000; this was not an unusual event in itself. It was one objective that had constantly to be kept in mind when selling to another company; one must ensure that their financial status was good. Many businesses were going under due to the recession and the precarious nature of the stock market. But this shortfall came during December, a month that was usually hit by lack of trade, due to the holiday period. It had been made even worse by the fact that prices of material had actually increased. As a consequence, the amount of surplus material available was very limited. Freddie knew that if they had another couple of liquidations, then they would go under themselves. His beloved Poseidon would be no more. He had to do something. Anything.

On reflection, what he should have done was to have sold the premises, moved to more modern and adequate accommodation and then he could have used the capital to bolster his business during this rough period. But he didn't. He put his business, his beloved Poseidon, for which he had worked so hard, up for sale. He began by looking at selling through agents, but they all wanted a huge slice of commission. He decided to sell direct and placed an advert in the newspaper – the Financial Times He had many enquiries, some were none starters. Many enquiries were genuine, but all going nowhere. Then he had one from an agent on the East coast, who offered to work for a lower commission if Freddie sold to their clients. To Freddie, it all seemed very reasonable at the time – provided he got what he wanted, lock, stock and barrel and provided they allowed him to stay on in a management position.

All seemed to be going well. The agent introduced Freddie to two characters, both of whom were well versed in corporate affairs. Awfully nice, public school boys. Perhaps this should have warned him. After all, many of us would not trust a politician further than we could throw them and this is the background of many politicians. However, Freddie was introduced to Messrs Fry and Steiner, the one a short character – a Jew, who never stopped talking or fidgeting. Freddie checked everything from the size of their bank balance, their credibility, to the colour of their underpants. Well, he thought he had checked everything, but it wasn't to be that easy, particularly when you take into account his state of mind.

Messrs Fry and Steiner were of course interested in getting their hands on the accounts. They were interested in Freddie settling his account with the company, to the tune of £14,000, for services that the company had supplied to him. This Freddie agreed to do out of the initial deposit, which they had agreed to give him, on the day of the signing of the contracts. They drove a hard bargain. But for once Freddie wasn't in a position to bargain, or shut the door on them. They, Messrs Fry and Steiner were the captive people, who were interested in buying Poseidon and at all costs, Freddie must do everything to save his beloved company. A company which would no longer be his!

Freddie realised he had waited too long. He was in such a situation that he had to sell, no matter what. He had no idea at the time just how much aggravation selling his company would cause to other people within the trade. People he knew well. People he had continued over the years to do business with, with whom he had built up a substantial amount of goodwill. Unbeknown to Freddie at the time, some of these would have bought Poseidon and now they took exception to the fact that he was selling the company elsewhere.

Freddie travelled to London to see his solicitors. The contracts were placed in front of him. Unfortunately due to his nutty as a fruitcake state of mind at the time, he had continued with his usual line of "I am Mr Bloody Wonderful, I can do it myself", not making allowances for his illness. He did not listen to the solicitors. He listened only to the sound of his own voice. This was the voice that kept pointing to the carrot at the end of the line, rather than the problems and difficulties of getting to the carrot on the way. It seemed that everyone else was after a slice of the carrot too, for by the time Freddie got to the end of it only the core was left and that, not in a very good condition.

The sale of Poseidon was sculptured so that Freddie would sign over all the shares, including those that Gabrielle had held. An initial transfer of £45,000 would be presented to him by banker's draft and he would sign over the effective control of the company to Messrs Fry and Steiner. A further £60,000 would be due to him in two, three monthly instalments in June and September.

He, Freddie would remain as Managing Director, captain of the ship; they would provide more contacts, making the company effectively bigger. They were to pump money into a successful, though ailing company.

Freddie paid back the £14,000 that he owed to the company. He paid £2,000 for shares that he took over from his previous partner. He also provided a further £10,000 to the company as an interest free loan. Freddie, in a way, still considered Poseidon to be his company. He was after all in control of sailing a ship for the owners, who should have been providing the fuel to make it go along.

Poseidon continued to trade. A breath of fresh air struck the company initially. Freddie felt good again. He felt bright and breezy. He had of course, to work for new mentors, not for the bank, but for two new bosses. But for Freddie, times grew a little harder. He had ensured that he had paid off all his debts, he owed nothing. In a sense he felt good about that, it was of course, less of a worry. However, it diminished the amount of ready funds that he had. Now, instead of running the shop entirely, having ready cash as and when he wanted it, Freddie, like everyone else had to wait for pay day. This in itself was an enormous blow to his system; life was going to be difficult.

Freddie needed money! He couldn't remember the last time he had been in this position; things had been so easy for such a long time. He decided to ask for his interest free loan back out of the company. No! That was the answer. As plain and simple as that – No! They would not let Freddie have back his own money, which he had put into the company, tax paid. An interest free loan, which he had given in good faith. However, they would come to a compromise with Freddie. They would let him have £1,000 a month provided that he get rid of his current car – a Ford Sierra Cosworth four by four turbo. This car was Freddie's current pride and joy; it was the fastest thing on wheels. It had the capability of doing 170mph. It was his perk for being management. It was his baby! But Freddie needed the money desperately.

An agreement was struck. The owners of Poseidon purchased a Ford Orion 1.6 for Freddie, in replacement of his "Cossie".

"Well, what do you think of the Orion then Freddie?" Steiner asked him one day.

Freddie was unforgiving and uncomplimentary. Did Steiner really think that this was an acceptable replacement?

"Well, it's marginally better than walking." Freddie replied snidely.

This stunned Steiner, who obviously expected grateful thanks from Freddie for buying him such a wonderful red, load of tat! For that was all that Freddie could think of at the time. Steiner shrugged his shoulders, turned and walked away. What their motive had been behind changing Freddie from such a powerful, awe inspiring emotive car, to one which was pace less and staid he never really knew, but they must have had their reasons.

Christopher Clarence Fry lived for graphs. He loved to highlight the relationship between certain sets of numbers; this is why he loved graphs. What the Karma Sutra was to sex, Christopher Clarence Fry was to graphs. He presented Freddie with graphs for sales, purchases, amount of telephone calls in and out – all superfluous information as far as Freddie was concerned. It was not his way of doing business. Freddie had brought Poseidon into the 21st century, setting up computer systems for stock control and so on, but now they wanted to go back to graphs and analysis and so on.

Freddie was a little closer to the scene these days, than he had been when Hammond had been around, so it didn't take him long to realise the game of Messrs Fry and Steiner. They were putting in high management charges. This was a shock to Freddie, but what could he do? Nothing, nothing at all. They were the people who owned the company. Freddie was only an employee. Messrs Fry and Steiner continued to put in excessive expense forms and management charges for doing literally very little.

One day, three months after they had bought the company out, they called a board meeting. An "Agenda for Sales" they called it. They wanted to know if Freddie could triple the sales within a specified time. He said he did not think he could deliver in the short time span they were effectively providing.

Did he feel then, that he was capable of turning the company around into profitability? Yes! Freddie felt he was confident in accomplishing that, providing the correct amount of investment in the company was made. Unfortunately, they had already run the company down. They had sold all the stock of the company. They had sold the bought sales ledger of the company. All that Poseidon had left was the property, its retained profits, its vehicles etc.

The bank had already begun to get a little edgy. Messrs Fry and Steiner had attempted to put a charge on the property for their management fees. The bank blocked their efforts and tried to do the same, albeit attempting to obtain the property of the company outright.

Messrs Fry and Steiner had been interested only in having a vehicle, which would pay them large sums of money, for doing very little. They weren't interested in debtors to the company; neither could they give a monkey's about the creditors of the company. Freddie couldn't give the answers that they wanted to hear at the board meeting. They had obviously been prepared, for the next minute a gentleman thundered into the boardroom, unannounced by either side. Freddie had no idea who he was, but it soon became very apparent. They had obviously neither known nor wanted the answers that he had given. The man was a liquidator, whom they had brought down from Manchester. By virtue of the fact that he had appeared about thirty minutes after the meeting had started, it had to be a preconceived idea, since he had travelled all the way from Manchester.

At a nod of the head from Steiner, the liquidator walked over to Freddie and said

"I am the liquidator of the company, you are dismissed, leave your keys to the car and go."

Well, being sacked is one thing, being sacked from your own company is quite something else and particularly when you are disabled and you rely on your vehicle to get from A to B. Was he, Freddie, being singled out? No, they were sacking everyone, everyone got the same notice. "Thank you and go." Everyone was to leave except Chris Hilditch, the bookkeeper, who it appeared had struck up a deal with Steiner. He had agreed that he would tie up the loose ends, if he was allowed to keep the computer system.

Rather good wasn't it? Within thirty minutes Freddie was without a job, without a car. Worse still, he had received less than a third of the money he had originally agreed upon with Messrs Fry and Steiner, in payment for the company. What a mug! What a prat! He had been duped again. Could the world really do anything else to him? The answer was a very big yes!

The inevitable creditors meeting arrived. Freddie was asked to take the chair. He was placed in the line of fire. The creditors in fact couldn't believe that a company, which had been as successful as Poseidon, which had risen to such heights in just fifteen years, could suddenly come crashing down so suddenly. Many of them put it down to Freddie's air crash and the state of his mental health. As the meeting finished, Steiner waddled over to Freddie, like an earthworm on its belly. He handed Freddie a brown envelope, telling him in an artificially friendly manner, that there was no need to open it there and then. Freddie did. Thankfully his solicitor was present. The envelope contained a High Court writ making a claim that would basically allow them to make more money out of Freddie. More money which he hadn't got. Freddie had no assets.

What Freddie hadn't realised at the time of signing the contracts, when selling his company, was that if the information they had received was insufficient, they could sue for the company's downfall. But without the aid of legal representation, he hadn't fully comprehended what this involved. As far as Freddie was concerned however, they had been given access to all the information they required from his previous accountants. How was he to know what information was needed? Well, it wouldn't have mattered either way, for they, Messrs Fry and Steiner, had worded the agreement in such a way, that there was no get out for Freddie and unfortunately no way out for his accountant either. In fact, his accountants' insurers ended up paying quite a considerable sum. Unfortunately for Christopher Steiner, he never lived to see any of this unearned income, since he died of a heart attack, just before the case was settled. Freddie remembered thinking at the time, how could he die in that way, since he didn't appear to have a heart. Perhaps understandably Freddie had no remorse for him.

Well, Freddie was unemployed. To many this would have been a considerable disadvantage. For Freddie, it meant that he could obtain legal aid in his fight against the writ that had been issued against him. However, he had to hire himself a good barrister, who made it clear to him that the contract that he had signed was pretty watertight and to the advantage of the purchasers and not to Freddie. Freddie in fact, had no other option than to settle with them. But with what? He had nothing.

Poseidon didn't exist anymore. It was purely fictitious. But Freddie Jones was still around. The creditors felt that someone should pay and quite rightly so, so why not Freddie Jones, Freddie Jones had a house, he had assets. Hadn't he? They didn't realise that he had been obliged to provide financial security to Gabrielle and the boys in case he permanently strayed.

For Freddie there had to be an option. Always in his life there had to be an option. This time the option was to go bankrupt. For the man who had everything, the best villas in Spain and Greece, holidays in Florida, he'd had everything, now he would consider anything. He had to face the possibility of bankruptcy, the ultimate profanity. But for Freddie it was no longer a disgrace, why should it be when he owned nothing anyway. If you don't have anything, you can't lose it. The one thing that he realised in life was that you can't beat anyone who is prepared to lose everything they have, whatever the cost. You just can't beat them. Materially, Freddie had nothing. He had lost everything – his company, his source of income, the love of his life. Yes perhaps she had been a possession too on reflection.

Freddie filed for bankruptcy. The bank manager, who had been a Jekyll and Hyde character, trying to please everyone, became a casualty. A loan and an overdraft were wiped off. He made a bit of a fuss, but it was no use. Freddie lost the use of his string of credit cards, including his cherished American Express Gold Card. He needed a job. He needed to support himself, to support his family. Fortunately, for Freddie, he still had connections in the metal trade. He contacted one or two people he had known for many years and supervised whilst working for the Pacific Metal Company. The irony of it was that they now owned their own company and he was to work for them. They were multi millionaires in their own right and they were prepared to give Freddie a second chance. He owed them a lot for believing in him.

Employed finally, he now had to live within his means, all because of the way that life had kicked him in the balls. He was just the average "Joe Bloggs" with a pay day. If ever, anybody was going to meet such a combination of devious and slick people, who were out for themselves, such as John Hammond, Fry, Steiner and the love of his life, it had to be Freddie.

But still he had his life. He still had a home, a car and a job. Most of all he still had his family.

15

The Venus Betrayal
and Life Goes On

Moving almost cautiously to the sofa he sat hesitantly on the edge. He felt almost android – looked human (or almost), felt human – sometimes, but knew that the body and mind were operating separately. The mind continued to reflect. It shouldn't have done really – not being android. But it did seem to compute and reason with historical events and attempt to find logic behind each occurrence.

He listened ...... The radio was blasting out a favourite of his – "Three Times a Lady" by Lionel Richie. What had happened to his princess? Where had she gone? For that matter where had his life gone? It was Beacon radio's "Our Song" spot and the DJ was thanking someone for sending in their story. He was the one that was being thanked......................

"And that one's for Freddie Jones and his ex lady. A special song for them both, that brings back memories of better times."

Helen had before their breakup, moved once more. The tiny maisonette, with no garden or back yard had been unsuitable for baby Luke and so she had decided a move was due. She found a modern town house, not far from her then abode. A pretty house, close to family and friends and Freddie still as much in love with her as ever, put down a large deposit. It was going to be his place too, so the idea of paying solicitor's fees, carpeting the house from top to bottom, buying a new suite, new cooker and fridge, the works in fact, seemed only reasonable. It seemed the right thing to do.

Freddie was spreading his time thinly between his family and Helen. The prospect of a new home with a new "wife" provided some excitement in the field of kitting the nest out. He would work all day, sometimes returning to Helen's house and would work hard on the decoration.

The bathroom had been in a hell of a state, until of course Freddie had refitted a brand new bathroom suite including a corner unit, gold taps, and the lot.

Returning home one day after work Freddie found a gianormous bouquet of flowers which had been delivered to Helen. He knew he hadn't sent them. He also knew it wasn't her birthday, anniversary and neither had she done a good deed for anyone who might be wishing to thank her. He was curious.

What could it mean? Who were these flowers from? He looked for a card within the flowers. He looked around on the side for the card. There was none. His curiosity getting the better of him, he continued painstakingly to search for a card, a clue, anything which might explain who had sent the flowers to Helen. He was beginning to panic, his heart missing a beat in anticipation of what he might find. He searched every room in the house, finally arriving in the bedroom and there in the bedside cabinet was a card.

You would have thought she would have been more discreet, more careful. Sharing a house with Freddie, she couldn't have hidden anything from him, not unless she destroyed the evidence. But she didn't, she left it there in full view, in the top drawer of the cabinet. Perhaps she had intended for Freddie to see the card, for him to find out? However, the flowers were in a sense still a mystery, since the pseudonym read "All my love VEE"; it was in fact from a Mr V Pwonka. When Helen arrived home she attempted to cover up her indiscretion, by stating that she thought the flowers were from Freddie. The card, he thought had quite obviously transferred itself into her bedside cabinet. But how many other things had he missed? He had been too busy to pay attention to what was going on, but there were other items which he considered were worth thinking about. An unbelievable row ensued, with Luke bawling his head off as their voices rose higher and higher in competition. Then the inevitable banging and slamming. Freddie knew, at this point, that the relationship had finally come to an end.

He felt he had failed utterly and it was all down to his mental state, to his short temper, his lack of memory. He most definitely was not the same person as before. He didn't look the same. He was horrendously disfigured. Was this the reason that Helen no longer loved him anymore? She was after all a very attractive girl and one who had everything going for her. Did she really need someone whom he considered to be suitable to take a lead role in one of the classic movies made by the Hammer House of Horrors? Had the previous ten years really meant anything at all?

Freddie sat, anger welling up inside of him. He had given so much to this girl, this woman of his dreams. He thought of their good times together. He remembered when he had moved Poseidon's base to Wolverhampton. It had been an ideal move for the business, particularly since it meant it was centrally located between Freddie's house and Hammond's house. Everyone had helped to paint the offices; they had had such fun, such laughter. Helen had managed to get paint everywhere.

Because of the move, it had meant that Helen would have greater difficulty in getting to work in the morning, so Freddie arranged to pick her up and drop her in the evening. It obviously had meant much more time together, which they were ready to grasp eagerly. After all, he had to be seen to support his employees. The distance would mean that Helen would get home late at night, but then so would he. As the summer and autumn matured they would stop on the way home.

He remembered now, the occasion they had stopped at the cornfield. Freddie had bought some late strawberries and a bottle of champagne, which he had kept, chilled in the fridge during the day. Helen had had a surprise for him also. She had stripped off and placed the strawberries one by one down her breasts, her stomach and finally to her most intimate of parts. He then ate them one by one, pouring the champagne over her body; he carefully and gently licked away the delicious combination of tastes – of champagne, of strawberries and of Helen. They made love there in the cornfield, just as they had on so many other occasions. The ghost of Helen still haunted him whenever he passed the cornfield.

He was devastated. He was angry. He, Freddie Jones, wanted revenge. If Vee Pwonka's wife didn't know about his dalliance, then by heck she was going to find out mighty quickly. Love and hate were on a collision course in his now tortured mind. The relationship was ended; Freddie had walked out, left there and then, leaving behind everything. But he wanted revenge, he wanted his pound of flesh and he would make sure he got just that. Her betrayal of him had made him decide there and then, that he no longer wanted her. How dare she feel she could be shared with someone else? He, Freddie would never share her with anybody and if he couldn't have her, then he would try damned hard to make sure no one else had her either.

Freddie was almost certain that it was someone that she worked with at a large computer company. She had little chance of meeting anyone else he thought. Following up his lead, he found that his suspicions were correct and went about finding the other man's address. The man and his wife had both lived in Stafford but had moved to Redditch. Freddie was utterly gutted, but wasted no time in ensuring that, that marriage was going to be a little rocky from this point on.

Separation decided upon, Freddie and Helen went about the difficult task of dividing up their belongings. Helen was to keep the house and a settlement of "maintenance". Freddie took back the car, which was after all in the company's name. He stopped her Access card and any other form of credit previously arranged. Now was the time for her to stand on her own two feet. Let's see if she could do it without Freddie. Well of course, she could. She had her new acquaintance by her side now.

Perhaps this was why his business had failed. The loss of his princess, the pain and anguish of the accident, the deceptive and Judas nature of those around him, all of these had contributed in some way to the loss of his beloved Poseidon. Of course, he had been too busy to give enough attention to those who owed him money as a consequence. Or perhaps, as his father had said it was a case of "Pride comes before a fall". He had been too proud, hadn't he? Perhaps, like all great civilisations, his downfall was inevitable. This was to be the end of his great nation, his empire.

Or was it the end? He still had his family! They had waited patiently for him. They were there for him through thick and thin. His guardian angel, Gabrielle was still there for him. In fact, his well being at that precise moment in time was all due to Gabrielle's patience and intelligence. It was Gabrielle who had put up with his moods, his nonsense. Gabrielle, who had put up with his tantrums, his fits of rage. Mentally, he had not been at all well – Gabrielle had been his stability.

Helen had had ten years of their life, ten years which Gabrielle had lost. Through it all Gabrielle had waited patiently, knowing that one day he would return. Gabrielle had not seen his loss of good looks, his loss of financial backing; she had not been concerned with the loss of Poseidon. All that had mattered to Gabrielle was that she had Freddie and the boys.

Freddie owed a great deal of gratitude to his wife in particular, but also to all those around him now who had proved to be true friends, people he had taken for granted. Had Freddie lost absolutely everything? Certainly not! Ask him now and he will tell you, he has everything. He has his family, his wife Gabrielle and his two sons. He had to give them his love and his thanks. He had to thank everyone including the doctors and nurses at the hospital who had struggled so hard to save his life. They who had struggled so hard once, they had saved his life, they had struggled to give him some sort of a semblance of life rather than leave him as a cabbage. He had to give thanks for the sunshine, the day, the night. Things that he may never have seen again if it hadn't been for these very special people. He had to give thanks for life – he had decided that it is special too!

Epilogue

During the last twenty years, the physical damage has in the main been successfully repaired, but the emotional destruction that Freddie suffered, from the loss of his beloved Poseidon and his princess have not.

Freddie has rebuilt his life financially; he still lives in a beautiful home with a swimming pool, drives a Porsche and displays the trimmings of success.

On analysing historical events and with the benefit of the exact science of hindsight Freddie now has the ability to question certain events and happenings.